Night
of
Wolves

The Paladins, Book 1

DAVID DALGLISH

Night of Wolves

BOOKS BY DAVID DALGLISH

THE HALF-ORC SERIES

The Weight of Blood
The Cost of Betrayal
The Death of Promises
The Shadows of Grace
A Sliver of Redemption

THE SHADOWDANCE TRILOGY

A Dance of Cloaks
A Dance of Blades
A Dance of Shadows (Christmas, 2011)

THE PALADINS

Night of Wolves
Clash of Faiths (Summer, 2011)

Night of Wolves

1

Jerico watched the river flow, the half-moon's reflection sparkling atop its waters, and from its darkness the creature emerged. Despite his training, despite discovering the crossing they'd used to harass the nearby village, the paladin felt his confidence falter.

"Be with me, Ashhur," he whispered as it swam toward him, its eyes gleaming yellow. He could only see the top of its head, a brief stroke of its arms, and the curve of its spine. Every inch was matted with wet fur, and it shone slick in the moonlight. One of its strokes pushed its head fully above water, and he saw rows of teeth before they sank below. It was those teeth that had devoured three children and their mother two nights before. Water dripped from its long claws as it stepped upon the shore. It was those claws that had torn the entrails from their bodies so it might feed.

A wolf-man, bastard creation of the god Karak and an unwanted relic of a war centuries past. It approached on two legs, its body hunched, its muscles taut and frightening. Jerico wondered how useful his platemail would be against those claws and teeth. The armor would do nothing if the creature grabbed his head and ripped it off his shoulders. He watched from the cover of trees that grew to the water's edge, his right hand clutching the handle of his mace. Slung upon his back was his shield, which he kept there, deciding he needed at least one surprise come the fight.

At the Citadel, he'd been trained to face all opponents with honor. An ambush, or stab in the back, was considered shameful. Jerico wondered if the same rules applied to the wolf-men. He'd never fought one before, only heard stories of their savagery.

Before he could decide, the creature stopped, and he heard sniffing.

"Man?" it growled, and Jerico felt the hairs on his neck stand on end. "Where is it you hide?"

With that nose, it'd only be a matter of time before it found him. Cursing his stupidity, he stepped from behind his cover, mere feet to the side of the wolf-man. It turned, and even with its hunched back, it still towered over him. His weapon shook in his hand as those yellow eyes narrowed when meeting his own.

"Leave now," Jerico said. "The village is under my protection, and I will kill you if I must."

The wolf-man laughed, its whole body shuddering. Its voice was deep and gravely. Jerico slipped his left arm back, grabbing the leather straps holding his shield. A single tug, and he'd have it at the ready.

"You want us imprisoned in the Wedge," said the creature, referring to the vast land beyond the river. "You wish us to starve and die. But there is food here, human. Food…"

It lunged, accompanied by a thunderous roar. Jerico stepped to the side, avoiding its charge. His mace connected with its chest, but hit so much muscle and hair it only tore free a small chunk of flesh. The creature's claws slashed his armor, scraping the metal with a horrific screech. Jerico swung again, this time aiming for its head.

The wolf-man moved with amazing speed for its size, ducking underneath the attack and then grabbing his wrist. With its greater strength, it held his weapon back, leaving him defenseless. Its drooling teeth snapped inward, aiming for his neck.

Jerico pulled the straps. Down came the shield, its steel shining a soft blue as he cried out to his god. The wolf-man's teeth snapped against it, and he felt his arm jolt at the contact. The creature howled, blood spurting from its nose.

"Back!" he cried, ramming with his shield. His heart hammered in his chest, and his eyes felt wide as saucers, but he'd survived the initial confrontation. The light of his shield grew, its power equivalent to the strength of his faith. The wolf-man released his arm, instead protecting its eyes from the light. With it dazed and on the defensive, Jerico tried to finish it off. His mace came in for the side of its head, but his confidence soon turned to panic. The wolf-man batted it aside with an arm, howled, and then attacked. The muscles in its legs were powerful, and it closed the distance with such speed he didn't have time to brace himself.

The creature shoved aside his poorly positioned shield and then rammed into his chest. Jerico flew back several feet, halting when he hit a tree. The air blasted from his lungs, and his vision swam from where his head struck the bark. Blood trickled down his neck.

"Your towers stop nothing," said the wolf-men as it stalked toward him, blood from its nose dripping across its teeth. "We come to feast, foolish man, and we are greater than you humans. We are not dogs. We are not orcs. You cannot stop us."

Jerico held his mace and shield before him, but his legs felt rubbery. He tried to focus, to anticipate the attack, but all he could do was stare at those yellow eyes and wonder how painful his death might be. Would he be alive when it ate him? His weight leaning against the tree, he vowed to fight until the wolf-man had no choice but to lop off his head.

"Greet me with open arms," he whispered to Ashhur as the wolf-man crouched down, preparing another lethal charge. But instead of leaping, it tilted to the side, and a pained howl escaped its throat. Dark fire swarmed across its body, and blood soon followed. It turned to run, one of its legs twisted at an awkward angle, but then a sword punched through its skull.

His armor was dark, the fire on his blades darker, so when Darius pulled his weapon free, he seemed a shadow blacker than the night itself.

"Ashhur won't need to take you yet," Darius said as the blood sizzled in the fire of his blade. His blue eyes twinkled. "And you can thank Karak for that."

Jerico slung his shield on his back and then rubbed his forehead. A chuckle escaped his lips.

"I didn't know you were following me."

"Neither did the wolf."

He suddenly felt ashamed for showing weakness before his rival, so he pushed off from the tree and fought through his grogginess. Gingerly, he touched the wound on the back of his head, but it felt shallow. He'd have a knot there for several days, but that was better than being a wolf-man's meal. Jerico joined Darius's side, and together they looked at the corpse.

"Do you still think the villagers are liars?" Jerico asked.

"Of course, but not about this. Even liars tell the truth from time to time."

"Such cynicism."

Darius laughed. He shook the crusted remains of blood off his weapon and then sheathed it. With its fire extinguished, it seemed Jerico could see easier in the darkness.

"It's merely truth, Jerico. I see the world as it is, you as how you want it to be. Doesn't take a scholar to know which of us will be right more often."

Jerico used his foot to roll the wolf-man onto its back. Its mouth hung open, and even dead, those rows of teeth gave him chills. He absently ran a hand along the deep grooves of his platemail.

"Did you hear what it told me?" he asked.

"I did. Who knows how many it meant. A pack could be five, or five-hundred. I suppose I should have left it alive long enough to question…"

Jerico pointed to the river. "We could cross and find out."

Darius laughed.

"Into their territory? Are you mad? I've never considered you paladins of Ashhur the brightest of men, but I figured you would at least have more sense than that."

Jerico shot Darius a wink.

"Ashhur calls the simple ones to do his work. We tend to accomplish more. Besides, if we go in the daylight, we could catch them sleeping. If they're crossing the river to hunt, they mustn't be too far."

"They've killed only four. That isn't a pack. That's hardly anything. This was a lone hunter, nothing more. Now, will you help me bring it to town, or must I do everything myself?"

Sighing, Jerico grabbed one arm, Darius the other. Together they dragged it across the leaves, through the forest, and to the town of Durham, so the people might see they had nothing left to fear.

The Citadel loomed before him, looking tall and proud in the twilight. As the sun continued to fall, an uneasy fear set over him. Spiderwebs of cracks stretched higher and higher throughout the Citadel's foundation. Fire burst upon the grass around it. Bones fell from the sky. As a great roar shook the plains, he heard a terrible crack, and then—

Jerico's eyes snapped open. His heart pounded in his chest. Despite the chill of autumn, his body was soaked with sweat.

Again? he wondered. *What is it, Ashhur? What is it you need to tell me?*

For the past week he'd had the same dream, and always it felt like it ended unfinished. Dread settled over him come the morning, and at least twice he'd thought to return to the Citadel to ensure everything was in order. But with Durham threatened by wolf-men sneaking out of the Vile Wedge and across the river to feed, he couldn't dare leave his assigned post.

As his senses slowly returned, he realized what day it was and groaned. He stayed in a small room of Jeremy Hangfield, the town's wealthiest occupant, the room freely given in exchange for protecting them from the various menaces of the wild. They were far from the great city of Mordeina and her guards, patrols, and roads. Here there were outlaws, bandits, and now, creatures of the Wedge. But fighting wasn't his sole duty, though sometimes he wished it was. Instead of putting on his armor, he donned his only pair of clothes that weren't bloodstained, a simple white tunic adorned with the golden mountain, symbol of his god. He clipped his mace to his belt but left his shield, feeling silly carrying it when not in armor.

His congregation was small, and they gathered in the town square. When he'd first come, nearly half the village had shown up, out of curiosity more than anything. As the days passed, his numbers had dwindled, now just a faithful twenty or so. Wishing he could be fighting wolf-men instead, Jerico preached best he could, often relying on songs to break the monotony. As he neared the end, he saw Darius watching him from the back of the crowd.

"Ashhur be with you all," Jerico said, ending his final prayer. As the crowd dispersed, Darius remained behind, his arms crossed over his chest. He wore a brown tunic with a black belt, the drab colors making his long blond hair stand out all the more. A smirk spread across his young face.

"Sometimes I wonder if Ashhur hopes to convert the lazy of Dezrel," he said. "Men who would be happy for an hour's sleep every third day, guilt free."

The comment stung. Twice Jerico had caught someone drifting off beneath the shade of a tree during his sermons.

"I guess I could scream and holler as if the world were on fire," Jerico said. "That just isn't my style."

Darius seemed unoffended. Jerico had witnessed the man's services, always held the day after his. The dark paladin was a far more animated spectacle, speaking with a passion he could never hope to match. He'd cry for strength, denounce cowardly sacrifice, and demand obedience in the face of a chaotic world. "Order," Darius would shout at the top of his lungs. "Bring this world Order!" Handsome, energetic, and passionate, his sermons gathered fifty to sixty men every time, a fact Darius never let Jerico forget.

"Your style should be what works," Darius said, tossing Jerico a waterskin, for he knew how draining such a performance was. "Not what you feel like. Perhaps you should attend a few more of my sermons. You might learn something."

Jerico drained half of it, then handed it back with a muttered thanks.

"How did Bobby take the news?" he asked, referring to the father and husband of those killed by the wolf-man.

"Come," said Darius. "I'll show you."

Together they walked down the dirt path, out from the village center. Wood houses sprang up on either side of them, fairly large due to the abundance of nearby lumber. At the end of the path was a post marking the entrance to the village. Hanging from ropes tied to its wrists was the body of the wolf-man.

In daylight it looked less fearsome. Its fur had dried out, much of it caked with blood and dirt. Flies buzzed about it, and it stank something unholy. All of its teeth were gone, and along its chest were at least twenty punctures new to Jerico.

"You let him mutilate the corpse?" he asked, though he already knew the answer. He just hoped he might somehow be wrong.

"Do you know a better way to move on after the death of a loved one?" Darius asked, lifting an eyebrow. "Here is his beloved's killer, and though it is dead, I still gave him a chance to exact his revenge. It accomplishes nothing, and after awhile, Bobby learned this as well. So I told him to take its teeth, and fashion a necklace so he might never forget."

"Bobby is a gentle soul," Jerico said, his stomach turning. He ran a hand through his red hair, his fingers gently touching the knot on the back of his head. It felt the size of his thumb. "He once paddled his daughter, then came to me to ask if it were right. Meanwhile, half this village wallops sense into their children at the slightest mistake. How could you let him do this?"

"Because he spoke to me of wanting to die," Darius said, yanking Jerico closer. "Would you counsel him love and forgiveness for the beast that ate his family? Would you promise him a better life in the world he wants to kill himself to enter? I gave him a desire for vengeance, and through that, a desire to live. You would have him remember his loved ones. Instead, I have him remember their murderer, and as long as he thinks of it, he is not wallowing in sorrow for himself and his family."

Darius let go of his tunic.

"Bobby's organizing a group of men to go into the Wedge," he said. "They want us to go with them."

"Will you?"

The dark paladin shot him a wink.

"I gave him his desire for vengeance. Do you think I'd abandon him after that? Question is, will _you_ come with us? I never am certain, given Ashhur's rather womanly tendencies. You'd scout for more, yes, but will you come for revenge?"

Jerico glanced into town, trying to decide. Of course Ashhur frowned upon revenge, but still, the entire safety of Durham might depend on their success. Besides, if something went wrong, many lives would be in danger. Could he turn his back on them?

"I don't like it," Jerico said. "But perhaps it should be done."

"They're just beasts," Darius said, slapping Jerico across the back. "Filthy, vicious beasts. We'll put them down, just like any other rabid animal."

Looking at the hulking form suspended by ropes, Jerico couldn't suppress a shudder.

"Any other animal?" he muttered as Darius walked away. Before he could decide for certain, he trudged back to the village. The streets were barren, for with autumn speeding by, the men and women were harvesting every bit of nut, fruit, and grain they could find or grow. He realized Bobby had not been there for his sermon like he usually was, and this fact squirmed in his gut like a snake. Needing to talk to him, he found the man's home, and sure enough, he was there instead of out in the fields with the others.

"Morning, Jerico," Bobby said. He sat on his porch in a small chair, his shoulders stooped and his leathery skin pale. His eyes had a glazed, distant look to them. In his lap, he held a necklace of teeth.

"Missed you at the square," Jerico said, leaning against the house. "Something the matter?"

"Sure is."

"Care to talk about it?"

Bobby finally looked at him as his fingers worked over the sharp edges of the teeth.

"Darius said you'd try to talk me out of going," he said.

"I'm only here to listen, friend."

"He said you'd say that too, but it'd be a lie."

Jerico rolled his eyes. "Lying's not my style."

Bobby grunted and looked away. He cut himself on one of the teeth, but if he felt it, he didn't let it show. Faint smears of blood started to spread across the yellow and white.

"I heard her screaming," he said. "I'd gone outside to piss, you know. That's all. And then, as I'm coming back, I hear her screaming. Just Susie, not my little girls or my boy. Do you think that means they died quicker? Maybe in their sleep? It didn't...it didn't..."

Tears rolled down his face. Determined to remain true to his word, Jerico kept silent, letting the man say what he clearly needed to say.

"It didn't even eat them, only my wife. Killed them for no reason, that fucking wolf. But Susie was alive when he was…eating. And it left me alive too, just looked at me and laughed. That damn thing *laughed*. I don't know if the one you killed was the one that came here. I'll never know. But I'll kill every last one I can find and hope each one is that bastard. And I'll laugh every time I kill one, Jerico."

"I'm sorry," Jerico said. "But this isn't right, and you know it."

Bobby looked up, and Jerico saw a rage there that frightened him.

"You think I care about what's right? I've lived right my whole life, and look what it got me. Someone ought to do something, so I will. No one else needs to see what I saw, and there ain't anything you can say to convince me otherwise."

Jerico stepped back. He felt helpless, overwhelmed by the man's grief. What could he tell him? That Ashhur worked in mysterious ways? That it was her time, her fate to have her belly shredded, her flesh ripped and swallowed while she was still screaming?

"I'll pray for you, Bobby," he said.

"Thanks, Jerico, but I don't think it'll do much good."

He stood and carried his blood-stained necklace into his house. When he shut the door, Jerico stood there staring long after. A hundred thoughts swirled through his head, but one in particular struck him with such certainty he knew he couldn't deny it.

He couldn't let this happen again.

His armor and shield were waiting for him in his room. There was a reason he carried them with him, a reason every paladin dressed for war. This was one of them. Come dusk, he'd join the rest. Come the night, they'd venture into the Vile Wedge, the land of orcs and monsters.

Night of Wolves

2

Gary Reed kissed his wife to cease her protesting. "I'll come back, I promise," he said, his hands brushing through her long hair.

He knew she wanted to believe him, but her tears fell all the same, and he wiped one away with his thumb.

"You better," she said.

Taking his sword, he left his home and walked to the town center. Fifteen men gathered there, a third of them holding torches. The rest held knives, pitchforks, and the occasional sword. They surrounded Bobby, who lifted a torch high above his head.

"It means a lot," Gary heard him saying as he neared. "Can't tell you all just how much, but it does. My Susie would be damn proud, I do know that. We can't let anyone else get hurt."

"Damn straight," shouted an older man named Trent, the closest thing Durham had to a blacksmith.

"We ain't sheep for them to hunt," said another, Gary recognizing this one as a fat farmer named Gruss.

"But you are sheep!" cried a voice separate from them all, and the crowd turned. Darius approached them, wearing his full plate armor, which seemed to soak in the light of the setting sun, giving it a frightful look. Painted in white across his breastplate was the face of a roaring lion. He kept his greatsword sheathed on his back, and Gary was thankful. He'd seen the dark paladin draw it only twice, but both times the fire that glowed upon it had made him uneasy. There was something unnatural about it, as if instead of giving light it stole it and hid it away.

"Sheep," Darius continued, for none dared challenge him. "That is, until you take up arms, as you have. This land belongs to the strong. It is weakness that lets men ignore the dangers about them, causes them to remain quiet in the face of injustice, to turn blind eyes to the chaos of this world. Tonight you do more than make his Susie proud. Tonight you do yourselves proud, your families, and your entire village! Let the wolf-men fear our wrath!"

The rest cheered, and Gary joined in. He still clung to his youth, his only child still in her second year, and he keenly felt the call for strength and pride. His sword shook in his hand, but it was from excitement, not fear.

"To the river!" cried Bobby, and the rest took up the call.

"To the river!"

Gary followed, imagining the cheer he'd receive if he were to behead a wolf-man. Bobby insisted there would only be one or two nearby, three at most. With the group of them, plus the dark paladin at their front, they would crush any of the monsters they encountered. Gruss liked to brag about the time he beat down two men from Ker unarmed, and Trent would go on for days about the jeweled bracelet he fashioned decades ago for an elven queen (whose name changed depending on how drunk he was), but who could top the bravery of him facing down a wolf-man and plunging his blade through its eye?

At the town's edge, a man slipped into the group beside Gary, remaining at the back. His red hair was long and well-cut. He wore silvery armor, heavy plate that made Gary feel naked in his simple farmer's clothing. At his hip swung a flanged mace, its grip leather, its metal dark. Across his back hung his enormous shield.

"Coming with us, Jerico?" Gary asked the paladin of Ashhur, unable to contain his excitement. "That's great. The wolves don't stand a chance now."

Jerico glanced down at his breastplate, and Gary saw the thick scratches across its front, dulling the shine. Some of Gary's excitement faded, replaced with a cold fear in his belly.

"I pray they don't," said the paladin, his face grim.

They arrived at the river. Gruss had agreed to let them take his boat, which he used for the rare trip south to sell extra crops to Ashhur's paladins at their Citadel. It seated four, but only Darius and two others crossed the first time, not wishing to overload it because of his heavy armor. Back and forth the boat went, taking several minutes for each trip. The river was wide and slow, its waters cold from the mountain streams that fed it. Gary hung back with Jerico, feeling safer at his side.

"We'll be able to kill them, won't we?" Gary asked as his nerves continued to grow. He felt fine when moving, as if filled with a sense of purpose, but now that he stood at the edge of a dark forest, watching a small boat travel back and forth across the Gihon, he felt his confidence falter.

"Darius and I killed one by ourselves," Jerico said, smiling at him. "And with all of you here, we can handle many more. But do not hope for combat, nor a chance to be a hero. Pray we all come home safe, and that your village will never see another one of those wicked creatures for many, many years."

Gary shifted uncomfortably on his feet, and he stared at the leaf-strewn ground.

"I just don't want to be a coward," he mumbled.

The paladin put a hand on his shoulder, and when he looked over, his eyes were kind and unafraid.

"I know you well enough, Gary, to say there isn't the slightest chance of that." He pointed to the shore. "Our turn."

Darius was organizing men into groups of five on the other bank when they beached.

"Jerico," he called, seeing their boat arrive. "Care to lead a smaller group, or would you rather remain up front with me?"

"Four groups should be enough," said Jerico. "Give me the smaller, and I shall watch our flank."

Darius pointed at Gary, the paladin, and a third bearing a torch. As he neared, Gary recognized him as the eldest son of his neighbor, a good lad named Dirk. He wasn't even fifteen yet.

"What in the Abyss are you doing here?" Gary asked him. "Your pa know you're out?"

Dirk blushed and refused to meet his eye.

"It won't hurt none," he mumbled.

"This ain't a deer hunt, boy."

"It's all right," Jerico said, pulling his shield off his back. A soft blue-white glow came over it, and immediately Gary felt his anxiety sliding away as it bathed over him. "Stay at my side at all times, Dirk, and keep your torch raised high. The wolf-men hate fire, and the light will hurt their eyes."

"Fight with honor!" Darius shouted. "I have their trail, and they will not dare run from our challenge."

Darius led the way, four of their strongest at his side, three wielding swords, one dual-wielding a torch and dagger. The other two groups marched behind and at either side. Jerico let them gain a bit of distance, then followed.

Gary felt his stomach twist into knots as they walked deeper into the Vile Wedge. It was said that the elven goddess Celestia cursed the land after the Gods' War, ruining the soil and stripping the land of wildlife. Gary didn't know if this were true or not, for this was his first time within. The grass was a pale yellow, though that could have been because of autumn's rapid approach, not any curse. There were no trees beyond the edge of the river, instead long, sloped hills looking barren in the growing moonlight. A thousand campfire stories ran through his head, and try as he might, he couldn't banish them. The Wedge was rumored to hold all kinds of villainous creatures, from orcs and goblins to the various animal-men, all twisted and formed to fight in the Gods' War. The wolf-men were one such creation, and of all the stories, he knew at least they existed. He'd seen the corpse tied at the town's entrance.

Deeper and deeper into the Wedge they traveled. Dirk grew increasingly nervous, but strangely, that made Gary feel better. His pride refused to let him show fear to a young boy approaching manhood.

"Maybe they've turned tail and run," he said.

"You sure Darius knows where they are?" Dirk asked. "I don't see no tracks."

Gary had looked himself and saw nothing in the light of the torch and Jerico's shield.

"Too many men ahead of us marching over them," Jerico said. "Trust him, and the others."

The river was but a distant shimmer when they heard the first howl of a wolf. It cut through him like a knife, and for the first time it seemed like Gary realized where he was, and what he was doing. He looked to his sword, an old relic passed down for four generations. He hadn't even sharpened it before coming out, ignorant of the proper way and not thinking to check with Trent. Men from the other three groups were certainly thinking something similar, for he heard them muttering among themselves.

A second wolf howled, this time from the opposite side.

"Careful, Darius," Jerico whispered. It did little to help Gary's already crumbling bravery.

They followed the lead groups into a gap between two gentle hills, their slopes hardly taller than a man. Their pace had slowed considerably, and Jerico lessened the distance between them and the others. When the howls came again, they echoed all around them. Gary swallowed, his mouth feeling stuffed with cotton. Beside him, the torch shook in Dirk's hand.

"Just two," Jerico said. "Either side of the hills. Don't panic. Stay with me, always with me."

Several of the men on the right cried out and pointed. Gary looked but saw only the hill. Another howl sounded, this one directly behind them. He spun, his knuckles white as he gripped his sword. The grass was empty. Someone from the lead group startled and was swiftly ordered quiet. More and more howling, and this time it was the men on the left who pointed. Gary caught sight of a dark blur, and he couldn't believe how fast it glided over the hill, vanishing on the other side.

Their groups halted, each one facing a direction. Moments later, Darius arrived and grabbed Jerico by the arm.

"Surrounded," he whispered. Gary stared back to the river, pretending he didn't hear and almost wishing he couldn't. Blurred shapes approached, hovering low to the ground. His heart crawled up his throat.

"How many?" Jerico asked.

"I don't know. Seven? Nine?"

"We need out of here, Darius. We aren't prepared, not for those numbers. Such a large pack—"

The wolf-men howled, and it came from all sides, merging together so that Gary couldn't begin to know how many there were. He imagined hordes of the creatures, enough to blot out the eastern grasslands, snarling and howling while drool dripped from their fangs...

Jerico grabbed his mace, and Darius drew his greatsword. Dark fire bathed its blade.

"We hold!" Karak's paladin cried.

"To the river, Darius, we must flee to the river!"

"No! We hold, all of you men, hold, we will hold!"

He rushed to the front, leaving the three there to defend. Jerico stood before them, his shield raised.

"Cry out if any come from the side," he told them. "Gary, stand firm, and watch for an opening. When you see it, do not hesitate. Do not be afraid. Kill it, and live."

"I don't know if I can," Gary said. The dark shapes grew more pronounced, three wolf-men running at horrific speed toward them.

"You will," Jerico said. Somehow a smile was across his face, and for the first time in their whole trip, he looked calm.

The wolf-men howled just before colliding with their forces, hoping to break the spirits of the defenders. Jerico stood firm, his legs planted and his shield in place. The three approached side by side, and in unison they lunged. Gary watched, feeling as if his feet were buried deep into the ground. Dirk, however, let out a cry and swung his torch. The rightmost wolf-man, having focused on Jerico, howled and turned its head away. Its slash went wild, and then it dug its claws into the earth to slow its momentum.

The other two slammed into Jerico. Gary expected him to fly back, unable to endure such power, but then the light of his shield flared. The wolf-men cried out in pain, and then it was they who fell back, one staggering on two legs, the other falling to all fours and snarling. It shook its head as if to clear away a fog. Jerico gave it no reprieve, stepping in and bashing its skull with his mace. It hit with a crack that made Gary's stomach turn.

The one that had sailed past returned, this time more carefully. Dirk waved his torch back and forth at it, as if shooing away a stray cat. At first Gary feared he'd been injured, seeing something slick on his clothes, but then realized the boy had lost control of his bladder. He couldn't blame him. From up ahead, he heard constant screams of pain, snarls of wolves, and chaotic orders combined with pleading.

"I'm no beast scared of fire," the wolf-man snarled at Dirk. Gary nearly felt his own bladder let go. The creatures could *talk?* Why had no one told him they could talk? Bobby had said it laughed at him, but he'd thought him hallucinating, caused by sorrow to hear strange things. The creature's voice was deep, grumbling. He realized the intelligence they must possess if they could communicate in such a way. Bobby had made it sound like they'd gone to hunt mindless monsters. But this…this…

The corded muscles in its legs tensed, and then it lunged. Dirk struck it with his torch, but he was young and outweighed thrice over. The torch bounced off the wolf-man's chest, causing no harm. The two rolled to the ground, Dirk's arms pinned, the wolf-man growling, its bared teeth reaching for Dirk's exposed throat.

Gary stabbed its side before it could. His sword sank halfway to the handle, then snapped when the creature twisted. Claws slashed across his face, the pain immense.

Blood blotted the vision of his left eye, and he clutched it with a hand. Be brave, he told himself as the wolf-man jumped off of Dirk. He saw only teeth. The dead one hanging in their town had had its teeth ripped out, he realized. He'd never have come if he'd seen them like he saw them now.

Its jaw closed on his shoulder; its weight slammed him to the ground. Warm blood spilled across his chest. He screamed.

"The Abyss take you!" Jerico cried, smashing its body with his shield. Gary saw the light stab into it, as if the glow were a dagger capable of cutting flesh. It released its grip on his shoulder, and he let out an involuntary gasp. Down came the mace, catching the retreating wolf-man across the snout. Teeth flew, and its blood sprayed across them both.

"We will feast!" it shrieked. Jerico's shield shone brighter, and amid his delirium, Gary thought he heard the paladin chuckle.

"No," Jerico said. "You won't."

The wolf-man charged, struck his shield once more, and then fell. Jerico's mace smashed the bones of its face, and it stayed down.

"Dirk?" Gary asked, trying to stand. But Dirk was fine, and he grabbed Gary's arm and helped him up.

"To the river," Jerico told the two as he turned to the battle beyond. "Run, and don't stop."

"Ashhur be with you," Gary said, leaning some of his weight on Dirk.

"You as well."

They stumbled west, between the hills and toward the Gihon. They'd taken no turns, the path Darius led them on perfectly straight, and soon they saw the river in the distance. Gary's shoulder burned, and every breath he took felt like fire in his lungs. Dirk didn't look much better, but guilty as he felt for burdening his wounded friend, Gary knew he could not run without aid. They glanced back only once, the torches looking like glowing dots in the distance.

It seemed like an eternity, but they reached the river and the waiting boat. Dirk helped him inside, then prepared to push it into the water.

"Wait," Gary said. His head felt light, but damn did it feel good to sit down. He clutched his shoulder and wished the pain would go away. Dimly, he wondered how badly the creature had scarred his face.

"No," Dirk said, realizing what he wanted. "Please, no, we can go…"

"We stay."

Dirk sighed, then shook his head.

"Fine. You're right."

They watched and waited for the first to show. A minute later, three men appeared, two relatively unscathed, but the third limped along in their arms, his left leg mangled and missing its foot.

"Hurry," Gary said, beckoning them to the boat.

"We thought you'd leave," said one of them.

"Never. Push us off, and then get in, Dirk. This boat'll float with five."

Out on the peaceful water, it seemed the fight was a hundred miles away. If not for the pain, Gary might have convinced himself it was a horrible, horrible nightmare. When they reached the other side, one of the men helped him out, and he lay against a tree beside the other wounded man.

"The others," Gary said, pointing back to the Wedge. He felt sleepy, and knew if he closed his eyes he'd succumb to it, but this was important. "You must…you must go back…"

Dirk was crying, his face wet with tears, but still he went to the boat and started to push.

"No," said a larger man. Jacob Wheatley, he realized. Jacob was always quick to argue, more temper than sense. But he seemed calm here, and he eased Dirk out. "I'll go."

He stepped into the boat, angled it, and began rowing.

Time grew slippery. Gary remembered the first boat returning, weeping men disembarking. He heard muttering, names listed off. Counting the dead, he realized. He wondered if they counted him or not. More men appeared, though he didn't remember their arrival. The water splashed the shore, and he wished to dip his hand in it. Suddenly he was thirsty, very thirsty.

"Gary?" someone asked. He opened his eyes, not remembering closing them. A young face hovered over him, blurry and unrecognizable.

"Get back," he mumbled. "I'm tired."

"Gary, it's Dirk. You got to stay awake. Gruss says you got to…"

Darkness, filled with the sound of water. Something touched his shoulder, and the pain awakened there. He opened his eyes and saw Jerico kneeling before him. White light shone from his hands, which pressed against his shoulder. His drowsiness faded, and the pain, which had been all encompassing, shrank down to something he could endure, something he could comprehend. Carefully Jerico wiped the blood from Gary's left eye with his bare thumb so he might see.

"Stand, Mr. Reed," he said, taking his hand. "You have a wife and child waiting for you."

Night of Wolves

3

When the light of morning shone through his window, Jerico winced. Every part of his body ached, and it felt like a pack of giants banged drums inside his forehead. He'd stayed up late into the night, praying over the wounded and offering them healing magic. Between him and the town's midwife, an old woman named Zelda, they'd sewn, bandaged and kept as many alive as possible. After that, the entire village had gathered in a prayer of remembrance, for they had no bodies to bury. Under the cover of stars, they mourned those the wolves feasted upon.

"Seven men," he muttered, rubbing his eyes. "We lost seven men. I hope you're happy, Darius."

He felt guilty saying it, but he also felt better. At least alone in his room he could grumble, mutter, and let his frustration show. Once in his armor and about the town, he had to be all forgiveness and prayers. Sometimes he enjoyed taking up his mace and smashing the head of an outlaw. At least he wasn't pretending about anything there.

But of course he also knew he wasn't being fair. Darius had taken them out to deal with a threat to the town. None of them could have foreseen how serious it'd be. After the battle, he'd spoken with all but Darius, who had stayed quiet and away from the others. Three wolf-men had attacked from the back, two from each side, and three more from the front. A pack of ten so close to the Gihon and the towers that guarded it? They'd killed six of the ten, and injured the remaining four. Given how unprepared they'd been, it could have been far worse.

"Jerico?" asked a voice on the other side of the door, followed by a gentle knock.

"I'm awake," he said, sitting up in bed and stretching his sore muscles. The door opened, and in stepped his host's pretty daughter, Jessie.

"Forgive me," she said, turning away and blushing when she saw Jerico wore no shirt. He chuckled, tossed on his tunic, and then asked her what was the matter. Something bothered her, he could tell. It was written all over her face.

"It's Bobby," she said, struggling to meet his gaze. Her eyes kept flicking to the floor, and her hands clasped behind her. "He...he hung himself last night. My father wishes you to pray over his body before we bury him."

The words knifed through Jerico, but despite the pain, he wasn't surprised. He'd seen the lingering sorrow and death in Bobby's eyes. Last night's excursion hadn't brought him the satisfaction he'd hoped for. Instead, seven of his friends had died, and many more suffered greatly. Again he thought of Darius, and wondered how the paladin was taking the news.

"I'll be there shortly," he said, sliding off the bed and reaching for his armor. Jessie started to close the door, then stopped. Her green eyes stared at him, and seeing the question aching to be asked, he prompted her to speak.

"Will Bobby go on to the golden land?" she asked. "Killing yourself...my father's always said the gods hate men who die a coward. Killing yourself's a sin, and to die sinning…"

His hand clasping his cold breastplate, Jerico stopped and frowned. He tried to decide what to say, what measure of truth would comfort her, and what he even knew himself.

"I don't know," he said. "I dearly hope so. He was a kind man. I'll pray for him, and pray that he's with his family in the hereafter. Surely Ashhur can fault no man for missing his loved ones as much as Bobby did."

"Darius said he deserved Karak's punishment."

Jerico pulled his armor over his head, shifted it, and then walked over to kiss the girl on the forehead.

"He speaks out of hurt," he said. "Pay him no mind. Now go, and tell your father I'm almost ready."

She smiled weakly, curtseyed, and then was gone. Jerico sighed.

"Damn you, Darius," he said, tightening the straps on his armor. "For once, couldn't you know better?"

It seemed half the town had gathered at Bobby's home by the time he arrived. Jerico's host, the tall Jeremy Hangfield, stood in the center, clearly in charge. He was a distant relative of a noble in Mordeina, and owned more land than the rest of Durham combined. Thankfully, the corrupting influence of his wealth never went beyond him and the tax man. The people treated him as their leader, lord in all but name.

"There you are!" Jeremy said, spotting him near the back of the crowd. "Come, Jerico, come! Darius has refused to pray over him, but Bobby was a good man, and he deserves no worse than any one of us here."

The way parted before him, and he stepped to the porch of Bobby's home. Inside, he saw a rope lying on the floor, having been cut from the rafter it'd been tied to.

Wrapped in a blanket was Bobby's corpse. His parents, their backs hunched, their skin deeply tanned by the sun, sat to the side, surrounded by their friends. Not far away, he saw the parents of Bobby's dead wife, and they looked too drained to cry. They'd lost all their tears the days before, suffering for the fate of their daughter and grandchildren.

Jerico knelt before Bobby's parents and took their hands in his.

"Is there anything you want me to say?" he asked.

The father looked at him, his eyes puffy and red.

"He wasn't his self when he did it. You know that, right? He'd never...he'd never do this..."

"He was already dead," said the mother. "Died when Susie did."

He kissed both their hands, stood, and then looked to the crowd. Some wanted comfort. Some were there to support their friends, and couldn't care less what he had to say. A knot grew in his stomach, and his tongue felt layered with sand. What could he say to them? He knew so little. At the Citadel, they'd taught him the words for funerals, what to say for the passing of men, women, and children. They'd never trained him to deal with the looks they'd give him, the near desperate desire for relief and comfort.

Jerico gave them what he could, and it felt like exposing a piece of himself as he spoke. He told them of Bobby's kindness, talked of the love of his family, and the grace he'd accepted from Ashhur. He said not a word of his suicide. Let the gods deal with that. When he finished, he gestured to Jeremy, who stepped forward, three men with him. They lifted Bobby into their arms and carried him out. They would bury him in the fields, forever to be a part of their village and their way of life.

Afterward, Jerico mingled, accepted compliments for his speech, and then searched for Darius.

He found him outside the town, sitting with his back to a lone tree growing atop a hill. The wind blew, and it felt wonderful against Jerico's warm skin. Speaking to the public always made him flush and feel like his neck were on fire.

"You weren't there for the burial," he said as he sat down beside him.

"Don't deserve it."

Jerico sighed. "Whether he hanged himself or not, he trusted both of us, and at least you could have—"

"Not him," Darius said, shooting him a glare. "*I* don't deserve to be there. He was hurting, and I led him out into the Wedge in hopes of aiding him. Instead, I made things worse. One of those that died was Bobby's best friend, Peck Smithson. How could he endure that?"

He leaned against the tree and thudded his head against the bark.

"I led us right into that ambush," he said, his voice growing quieter. "The tracks were so obvious a child could have followed them. I should have known something was wrong. The people of this village aren't fighters. They're farmers, shepherds, and herdsmen. Now more are dead, the village suffers for the lack of hands, and the one I sought to help spent the night hanging from his ceiling by a rope."

"Yeah, you really messed up, didn't you?"

At Darius's glare, Jerico chuckled and smacked his shoulder.

"If our gods agree on something, it's that we're all human, and all make mistakes. Let it go, Darius. You did what you thought was right. Next time, don't let your guilt keep you away. I'm tired of dedicating all the burials around here. Oh, and don't give a damn sermon about the punishment awaiting a loved one who died mere hours before."

"You would have me lie about my beliefs to make them feel better?"

"I'd have you show a measure of tact and talk about anything else in the world for the next few days. Surely you can grant me that?"

Darius sighed. "Very well. The least I could do for what remains of his family. It's not like I want it to be this way, Jerico. The rules we live under are harsh, and not everyone will meet them, but truth is stone, unbending, unmoving. That is the way of Order."

Jerico stayed silent, not wanting to discuss theology. Instead he gestured east, toward the distant river.

"What do we do about the wolf-men? From what I gathered, it was a pack of ten that attacked us. That, plus the raids across the river worry me to no end. They've found a gap in the towers, and Durham's right there in the way."

"We killed more than half," Darius said. "And that was with them having the advantage. Do you still think they'll press us?"

"How do we know it was half?" Jerico asked, voicing the fear that had been nagging at him. "We were within the Wedge only a little while. How many might be gathering? We could have stumbled upon a single hunting party, not the entire pack."

Darius shook his head. "That can't be. That would mean a pack of fifty or so, maybe more. It's been years since any packs of that size. The elven scoutmasters keep them thinned and at war with one another, and someone that strong usually finds an arrow in their neck."

"Except the elves are gone," Jerico said quietly. "We cannot take any chances. Let us request aid from the towers, together."

"We can handle this," Darius said, his stubbornness and pride returning.

"Whether we can or can't, I'd rather we err on the side of caution. Trust me on this?"

Darius sighed.

"Twice now I agree to your demands. I must be bothered by this more than I thought."

"Good. It's a welcome reminder you're as human as I am."

Jerico gave him an exhausted grin, and the dark paladin relented to his good humor.

"Write your request," Darius said, standing. "And I will sign it."

"Where are you going?" asked Jerico.

"I have a family deserving my apologies," said Darius. "Not that it's your business."

Jerico leaned against the tree, closed his eyes, and enjoyed the weather. Slowly he felt his tension drain away, and once renewed, he returned to Durham to write his letter to the lord of the Towers.

R edclaw waited at the head of his pack for his scout to return.

"He will see little in this daylight," said Bonebite, his most trusted warrior. His fur was faded with age, but he'd feasted upon more fallen foes than anyone else in his pack.

"The orcs are slow and stupid," said Redclaw. "They will not expect us to attack while the sun burns the sky."

Bonebite snorted. "Does the mighty Redclaw need the help of surprise to kill a few runty orcs?"

Redclaw bared his teeth, both smile and threat. Bonebite had once vied for the position Redclaw now held. They'd fought for the honor, but instead of killing him as was custom, Redclaw let him live.

"Wolf should not kill wolf," he'd declared, his first law of the pack. He'd killed plenty enforcing the rule, but none in the pack were intelligent enough, or brave enough, to point out the contradiction. Bonebite had resented him for the longest time, but Redclaw treated him like the proud warrior he was, and after a time, the wily old wolf had accepted his role, and appeared to even appreciate the younger warrior's skill and leadership.

"Whenever we fight, we must win," Redclaw said, turning back east and squinting in search of his scout. "Why let orcs fight fair against us? They deserve nothing. They are food."

"The fight weans out the weaklings," argued Bonebite.

Redclaw glared at him. Bonebite's snout was covered with scars, his nose nearly white with them instead of its original black. One scar ran straight across his eye, the hair around it never growing back.

"Even our weaklings are stronger than the best of man and orc," he said. "One day you will fall, Bonebite. Would you have me hail you a warrior, or a weakling, when we consume your flesh?"

"Neither," said Bonebite, and he let out a laugh. "I will be too tough and dry by then. You will choke."

"I'll moisten your flesh with the blood of men. Now quiet. I see my scout."

"I see only the fire in the sky."

"Then your eyes already succumb to the weakness of age. I hope the rest of you is not the same."

Bonebite growled but said nothing. Racing along the plain came Redclaw's scout, running on all fours. His tongue lolled out the side of his mouth.

"They've come from a hunt," said his scout, the aptly named Swiftheel. He panted and reached out his hand. A nod from Redclaw and Bonebite gave him a dried stomach full of water.

"Better," growled Swiftheel after drinking. "The orcs are tired, and will soon be fat and lazy from eating. The time is right."

"How many are they?" asked Redclaw.

Swiftheel let out a little yip, as if amused his pack leader thought their numbers would matter.

"Four times I counted to fifty."

"Has their camp been moved?"

"No, they stay in the ravine. They must feel safe there."

Redclaw let out a howl, alerting the rest of his pack.

"Their safety is their doom," he snarled. "We will seal both sides. Tonight we feast on the flesh of hundreds of orcs, brethren! With me! To the bloodshed!"

He raced off on all fours as over a hundred more gave chase behind him. The distance was a little under three miles, but they crossed it swiftly. In the cool of night they could run forever; it was only the fire in the sky that made them pant. If they had not been outnumbered, he might have held the raid at night, but he had to hit them unprepared. He had ambitions far greater than the Wedge could offer, and to fulfill them, he needed a pack large enough to endure. When the howls sounded across the land of humans, he wanted them to know fear.

The ground steadily grew rockier, and Redclaw slowed his pack. Up ahead was the ravine, dipping down into the land like a great scar. The orcs had built a wall at either entrance, but the camp was new enough that they had not yet reinforced it, nor built rudimentary towers to keep watch at its top. He didn't know why they had encroached his land. Perhaps they fled one of the other orc tribes, or they had been scattered and forced their way by the other vile races within the Wedge, the hyena-men with their short, thick claws, or perhaps the bird-men with their cruel beaks.

Whatever the reason, it didn't matter. They'd come into Redclaw's ever-expanding territory, earning their fate.

A quick growl, and Bonebite veered to the side, leading half his pack to curl around the ravine and assault from the rear. Redclaw slowed his pace, wanting to give them time to set up. They would hit at once, crawling over both walls and shredding their camp before the orcs could organize a defense. They came from the west, using the depth of the ravine as a shield against watching eyes. No one kept watch, a stupidity that might explain why they had been forced to flee in the first place. No doubt an orc or two stayed at the walls within the ravine, but they would have only a moment's notice when the wolf-men came rushing in.

Redclaw stood on his legs and lifted a hand. The rest of his pack pulled up, and he heard their panting. A few nipped at one another, clearly on edge.

"Calm," he growled. "Save your bites for the orcs."

They endured the daylight and waited, every muscle tense. When the signal howl came from the opposite end of the ravine, they answered in unison.

"For the blood!" Redclaw cried, leading the charge. They stormed into the ravine, toward the wooden wall blocking their way. It was designed against other orcs, no doubt who they thought their greatest enemy. But the wood was thick, rough, and it yielded easily to their claws.

Cries of warning came from inside, but no spears thrust at them, no cowardly arrows sailed through the air. Redclaw scaled the wall, paused atop it, and scanned. Orcs were scurrying about, grabbing swords and shields. No line had formed yet, though it seemed like the greatest force gathered in the center, no doubt where their tribal leader hollered in panic.

Three orcs were below him, the spineless lot abandoning their posts in flight. With a push of his enormous legs, Redclaw dove upon two of them at once, his claws shredding their flesh. He let out a howl, and he felt himself falling into the wild warrior beast that lived deep within him. The planning done, the fight begun, he allowed himself to give in.

At first, it was too easy. They raced through the many tents, clawing and biting at any nearby. Mostly it was the old or weak, those unable to fight. Hiding inside the tents, they acted as if they would be safe there. They were not. Blood soaking his fur, Redclaw killed everything that moved, and he drank his fill. From the far side, he heard the roars of Bonebite's group, and more worrisome, howls of pain. The orcs had finally begun to fight. Furious that he had missed the initial confrontation, he tore through the tents, calling for his pack to join his side. Forming a wedge of nine, they thundered toward the large center of the camp, where the orcs had chosen to make their stand.

Redclaw dove into where they were thickest, unafraid of their thin spears and cruel swords. His claws were sharper, his muscles greater. Even the orcs, tall and strong compared to most races of Dezrel, were puny compared to him. He descended upon one, tore out its throat with a quick snap of his jaw, and then spun to his right. He slashed at the wrist holding the blade swinging at him, and the blow lost all strength when it hit, the blade unable to pierce the thick hide beneath his black coat of fur. A quick swipe, and the orc fell back, blood gushing from its torn throat.

All around he heard the sound of fighting, and at his side were his trusted pack, tearing into the orcs as if their armor were butter, their weapons toys. Still, the orcs were stubborn, and their spears were the worst. Redclaw caught sight of one of his best warriors howling, a spear embedded deep in his breast.

"Back!" he cried. "Circle!"

They began running, both his group and Bonebite's merging together in a river of fur and muscle. The entirety of the orc camp huddled in a circle, everyone else having been massacred. Redclaw guessed at least sixty within, maybe more. They kept their shields high, and their spears poking past the front lines. Deep within, he heard the angry cries of an orc chieftain.

Redclaw led the circle, the rest following his lead. He dipped them closer, then pulled away, never letting the orcs know for certain where the ring would stretch or shrink. The nervous orcs at the front lashed out several times, always missing, always finding their arms grabbed or their weapons snatched from their hands. Once they fell into the circle, they never stood again. Trampled under the pounding feet, they could only cry out until dead.

Redclaw howled, and his pack took up the call. The orcs looked ready to break. He could smell the fear on them, and it was strong. His next howl was an order, and his pack obeyed with perfection he was immensely proud of. Leading the way, he lunged into a gap of orc shields, batting aside a wild thrust of a blade. He didn't fight the outer wall, instead shoving through, trying to crack their ring. The rest of the wolves did not attack as the orcs expected. Instead they continued to circle, pouring into the gap opened up by Redclaw. They cracked the orcs like an egg, pushing deeper and deeper into their center. He had almost reached their chieftain when the orcs on the opposite side, realizing they were no longer surrounded, turned to flee.

The battle belonged to the wolves.

Redclaw drank the blood of their chieftain as the rest of his pack hunted down the fleeing orcs. Only the hyenamen could run faster than his kind, he knew. The slaughter would be complete. He stood atop the dead body and roared his victory. Bonebite joined him moments later, sporting a fresh new scar across his chest.

"Lucky bastard," said Bonebite, seeing Redclaw's eyes analyzing the wound. "I tore his head off for it."

"Gather our dead," Redclaw told him. "It is time we honor them."

Twelve wolf-men had died in the attack, a far cry from the two-hundred dead orcs. Many others were wounded, but his people were strong, and he knew they would endure without complaint. They gathered the twelve together, laying them in a line side by side. Redclaw scanned them, searching for the strongest. Recognizing the corpse of a young, hot-tempered wolf-man that had gone by the name of Bloodgut, Redclaw walked over to it and then knelt on all fours. He was the one he'd seen struck by a spear.

"To our glorious dead!" Redclaw cried out, plunging his claws into Bloodgut's chest and tearing out his heart. He shredded it in his teeth, the blood sweet across his tongue. With that, the rest descended upon the bodies, all strength of the pack preserved and redistributed throughout. The twelve were not enough to sate their hunger, though. Each wolf took the body of an orc, some still alive, and flung them over their shoulders.

"Let us return," Bonebite said, two orcs across his back. "My pups will be hungry."

They walked back on just their two hind legs, the journey much longer. They walked in victory, though, so they bore their aches and the light of the sun in good humor. At last they reached their camp. Only the pups remained, those not strong enough to fight. The women had come with them on the attack, and they had performed well during the slaughter. Redclaw dropped the orc he carried. His two pups approached, their arms lightly touching the ground for they were still learning to walk upright.

"Eat well," he told them, proud of their size. Already he knew they would outgrow him. Come the day they feasted on his remains, they would fight amongst each other, the winner sure to be a great and powerful pack leader. Maybe they would surpass his accomplishments. He hoped they would.

As the rest arrived, Redclaw saw that it was not just children at the camp. A smaller wolf-man waited in the camp's center, kneeling on his haunches in a display of humility. Redclaw recognized him as Yellowscar.

"Why have you come?" Redclaw asked him.

Yellowscar averted his eyes, his ears pulled back against his skull.

"Rotfur crossed the river," said Yellowscar. "He went against our wishes, and he feasted on the blood of a human woman. The second time he crossed, he never returned."

"Damn him," growled Redclaw. "Better the humans took him, for that fate is better than what I would have given."

"It is worse," said Yellowscar. He pressed his stomach flat against the ground. "A group of humans ventured into the Wedge, led by two terrible men, one with a sword of fire, the other a shield of light. We killed many before they could retreat, but we lost six of our own."

Redclaw felt anger flare through his veins. He'd led an assault on two hundred orcs and lost twelve, yet Yellowscar and the rest of his scouts lost half that to a mere party of *humans?*

"They will know we are coming," Redclaw growled, his voice deep and dangerously quiet. "They will send for men from the towers, armed with metal skin and cowardly bows. You let Rotfur's bloodlust go unchecked. I said watch, and see if the waters are safe to cross. You fail me, Yellowscar."

"I know," Yellowscar said, his snout pressed to the dirt.

Redclaw grabbed him by the neck and hoisted him to his feet.

"Wolf does not kill wolf," he said, staring into Yellowscar's eyes. "You will pay back your mistakes. When the men come down the river, you will be ready, and you will be the one at the front of the attack."

"I understand, pack leader."

Redclaw dropped him and ordered him away. His rage still beat through his veins, and he knew his vow might be tested should the young scout remain in his sight. Fearful for his plan, he looked back at his pups. They deserved far better a home than the Wedge. Beyond the Gihon there was plentiful game, creatures they saw rarely. Deer, with meat so soft. Rabbits, which squealed when biting into their tender flesh. Streams, with water clean and light on the tongue…

"We will escape your prison," Redclaw growled to the west, imagining the legion of humans that would quake with fear at the sound of his howl. His words were a promise, a vow to which he had sworn his entire life. "We will escape your blades. It is we, the wolves, who will feast."

4

Despite the respect his men showed him, despite the importance lauded on him by the nearby villages, Sir Robert Godley knew his position was an insult, the best King Marcus Baedan could think of for one of his station.

"The seer says this winter will be a harsh one," said one of his lieutenants and closest friends, a slender man named Daniel Coldmine.

"Who, that old crone in Dunbree?" asked Robert, staring out the window of the great tower overlooking the Gihon. "She also said I'd fall for a lovely lass come my fortieth birthday, but she'd only betray me. Been a decade past that, and still no lass."

"Maybe she meant King Baedan," Daniel said, joining him at the window, a smug grin on his face. Robert chuckled. Perhaps Daniel was right. He looked down at his portly body, remembering a time when it had been all muscle, his heavy fingers calloused from the daily wear of his sword's hilt. But that had been before the disastrous defeat at the hands of the elves years before. They'd chased their kind out of Mordan for good, but at the southern bridge leading to Ker, the elves had sent their greatest to make their stand. The magic they'd wielded was immense, godlike powers he still saw in his nightmares. Boulders of ice the size of houses had crashed through his ranks, and fire had rained from the sky, each piece of burning hail bigger than his fist.

"Baedan's no lass," Robert said. "He's just a spineless bigot, Karak curse his name."

Daniel pointed to where smoke burned in the far distance inside the Wedge.

"A hunting party, perhaps?" he asked. "Orcs? Or have the hyena-men finally learned how to make fire?"

"No matter," said Robert. "It's too far away. I won't lead what few men I have in a hopeless chase of distant smoke."

"There was a time when we would have ridden across those dead plains on a hundred horses," Daniel said, a wistful look coming over his face. "The damned creatures feared the very sight of the Gihon, our boats and our towers. What happened?"

Robert turned away from the window and leaned against the stone. Closing his eyes, he sighed. During that disastrous attack against the elves, he'd pulled back his men, refusing to continue. They'd lost thousands trying to kill a mere ten. There would be no victory, no revenge. The fight had lasted another six hours, and when Marcus heard of his retreat, he blamed him for the deaths, as if his cowardice had allowed the elves to endure as long as they did. But Robert was also the hero of Dezerea, and it was his strategy that had burned the elven capital to the ground. Unable to punish him how he wished, instead Marcus had sent him to the wall of towers.

Year after year, the king had denied requests for supplies and soldiers. Their boats grew worse, their weaponry chipped and dull no matter how often they polished and shined it. They'd been forced to beg donations from the nearby villages, for Baedan's coin was not enough to feed them all. Their role in patrolling the river, protecting the lands from the various creatures of the Vile Wedge, ensured the local populace aided them whenever they could. Robert's muscular body had thickened as the tedious years rolled on. His calluses had vanished, his black hair grown long and gray, and his finely honed reflexes had faded away into the dusty corners of his mind.

"You want to know what happened?" Robert asked. "I was put in charge. That's what happened. Marcus will bleed us with the patience of a spider, until at last we are so weak something gets through. He doesn't care how many die, so long as he can strip me of my title and exile me in shame."

Daniel grew quiet, and he looked to the distant smoke with new worry.

"We're not so thin," he said. "We can stop whatever those savages send at us."

"Here, perhaps," said Robert. They were within his study, and he walked across the room and gestured to a map of northern Mordan. Drawn in exquisite detail were the towers placed alongside the Gihon at thirty to forty mile intervals. The distance grew the closer they came to the Citadel, for the paladins aided them in guarding the lower section of the Gihon, where it met the Rigon, forming the lower V part of the wedge. Robert gestured to the various towers, all named after the colors they were drawn in.

"Tower Red and Silver are at a tenth of their full capacity," he said, pointing at the two nearest to theirs. "Green is down to a single horse, and I have none left to send. The best I can hope for is a wealthy farmer donating one to us. Gold's foundation is cracking, and no matter how often I request a mason from Mordeina, Marcus only responds with vague promises. At the far end, Violet is all but unmanned, the paladins of Ashhur graciously patrolling its waters for us. Most of our troops lack training, don't try to deny it. We're a rotting fence penning in a herd of bulls. One of these days those bulls will realize it, turn their horns our way, and smash through."

"What of the Blood Tower?" asked Daniel. "How are things there?"

Robert forced himself to smile. Blood Tower was his, the base of command for the entire wall.

"Blood has the finest soldiers Mordan could hope for," he said. "And I hear they won't quit no matter how terrible their situation becomes, and never will they let the creatures cross the Gihon."

"That's what I thought," Daniel said.

Someone knocked at the door, and Robert ordered them in. A younger lad, an orphan volunteered into their service from a nearby village, stepped inside, bowed his head, and offered a small scroll. Robert took it and dismissed him.

"More promises and gifts from Mordeina?" asked Daniel, his voice thick with sarcasm.

"No," said Robert, furrowing his brow. "It's from Durham."

"Durham?"

Robert pointed on the map. It was an unnamed dot in the lengthy space between towers Bronze and Gold, not far from the river.

"Says wolf-men have been crossing the Gihon. Damn fools, they even went into the Wedge to try stopping them. They killed six, but say at least four remain. Now they want our help in case there's more."

"Sounds like they're capable of handling this themselves," Daniel said.

Robert handed him the scroll so he could read for himself.

"They went into the Wedge and found monsters," Robert said, returning to the window. "Nothing surprising about that. It says only a single wolf-man actually entered their village, and it was slain. Starvation probably drove it across."

"It's far from either tower," Daniel said, glancing back at the map. "I guess our boats don't go there except maybe once a month. Still, worrisome that there'd be so many bunched together."

"They're probably lying about the numbers they found, just to get us to help them."

"I doubt that. It's signed by two paladins. Shit, one's Ashhur, and one's for Karak."

Robert raised an eyebrow. He yanked the scroll out of Daniel's hand and scanned the bottom.

"Tan my hide," he said. "You're right."

"If something can get a paladin of both gods to agree, I'd say it's serious."

"Damn it. Two paladins, and they can't defend themselves?"

"Those two might be the only reason they killed the ones they did," Daniel pointed out.

"Fine. If you're so overcome with boredom, take a squad and go. It might do some good to instill a bit more faith in us. And give Sir Lars an earful when you pass through Bronze. That's his stretch he's supposed to be guarding, and don't let him tell you otherwise."

Daniel struck his breast with his fist and bowed.

"I'll tell you of all my legendary conquests when I return," he said, grinning.

"You're not much younger than I," Robert said, laughing. "I'll be impressed if you even get blood on your sword."

"Perhaps not younger, but I'm not as fat, either," Daniel said, ducking out the door before Robert could respond with the rightful blow to the head he deserved.

⧫

The week passed, and the people of Durham moved on best they could given their losses. No wolf-men crossed the river. Jerico and Darius resumed giving their respective sermons, though Jerico noticed his numbers had grown by fifteen or so, while Darius's dwindled. No doubt many still bore grudges at his pain-fueled condemnation of Bobby's fate. All the while, they waited for the message they'd sent upriver by way of tower Gold to be received, and the response to be given.

On the eighth day, as Jerico toiled in the field, he saw a man in silver armor approach from the distance. Straightening up, he stretched his arms and waited.

"Jerico?" asked the man as he arrived. He was older, with a white, well-trimmed beard. His small eyes looked Jerico up and down. "Or perhaps I am mistaken?"

"I am he," Jerico said, offering his hand.

"Strange to see you half-naked and working a field."

Jerico chuckled. "On days with nothing to preach, I like to help with what I can. It is the least I can do for what they've given me."

"You bring them truth and salvation. The least they could do is feed you and give you a roof over your head," said the man.

"Might I have your name?" Jerico asked, the man seeming familiar, but only a little.

"I am Pallos. I've come from the Citadel to observe your progress."

52

Jerico laughed. "Well, I've done about a quarter of this field, and should have another quarter done by sundown…"

Pallos's glare showed that he was not amused.

"Right. Sorry. I'm actually glad you're here. Let me go tell Jeremy he'll need to send someone over here to replace me, and then we can return to the village."

"I'll be waiting," said Pallos, saluting with a mailed fist. As he walked away, Jerico wondered just how far Pallos had his sword shoved up his ass. Of course, such thoughts were hardly worthy of a paladin, but as he hurried to where Jeremy overlooked the rest of his workers, he figured that Ashhur might not only forgive him, but probably agree over the matter.

Pallos sat in the shade of a tree not far from the village square, drinking from a waterskin. Jerico joined him, having taken a quick detour to his room to throw on a shirt. It felt grand while out in the field working, but once at rest, his body slick with sweat, the air turned uncomfortably chill.

"I hope you had a pleasant ride here," Jerico said, sitting down beside his superior.

"Pleasant enough, though I must apologize for my mood. I have lost a dear friend; we all have. That is why I have come."

"Who?" asked Jerico.

Pallos leaned his weight against the tree, and he looked rather uncomfortable about the whole matter. His eyes watered, but the man's self-control was too great for such displays of emotion.

"Mornida died of a sickness. Sorollos has replaced him as High Paladin. I've been traveling north informing all of our men in the field."

Jerico crossed his arms and frowned.

"A good man," he said. "Though I doubt I knew him as well as you. But we are strong, and will endure the loss."

"Sorollos is a young man, but his faith is great. Still, I miss Mornida's leadership. But enough of that. He is with Ashhur now, and we have worldly matters to discuss. I spoke with many villagers before coming to you, Jerico, and what I heard distresses me greatly."

Jerico knew where this was headed, but he asked anyway.

"About what?"

"Your friendship with a paladin of Karak. What is his name, Darius?"

His mouth felt dry when he responded. "Yes."

"We knew he was here when I positioned you in Durham. You were to counter his doctrine and free the villagers from his lies. Instead I hear of you befriending him, even spacing out your sermons so the people here may attend both."

"I thought it best to let them hear both our doctrines, and let them see the truth of Ashhur's wisdom by comparison."

"Serving Ashhur is a *choice*, Jerico." Pallos frowned at him, and Jerico felt like he was back at the Citadel, being reprimanded for a wrong answer. "People cannot serve both Karak and Ashhur, and it is foolish to give them the chance to do so here. Karak's darkness will not be defeated in such a way. You do not stop the charging bull with flowers. You kill it with a sword."

"Darius is a good man, Pallos. He worries about this village as much as I."

"Good man or not, he serves a lie, and in his ignorance, he will damn the people here. Challenge him. Watch your friendship crumble when you stop acting as if his beliefs are worth hearing."

Pallos looked at him, honest sadness in his eyes.

"He serves Karak, and come a time, Karak will call him to betray you. That is when you will see your worth to him."

Jerico turned away and refused to acknowledge him. The silence dragged on, awkward and uncomfortable. At last, Pallos put a hand on his shoulder and squeezed it gently.

"Do not be mad with me, Jerico. I am old, and have seen the evil this world fosters. I only say this because I fear the hurt that will befall you. But let us talk on other things. Your shield...is it still your beacon? I would very much like to see it."

Jerico welcomed the excuse to leave his presence, if only for a little while. He seethed at such condemnation of someone like Darius. Sure, the man had his faults, but didn't everyone? But he'd been there beside him, bleeding and fighting for the safety of the village. He called the men to be strong, the women to be faithful, for all to follow laws that, while strict, often seemed fair. They were both young, and they understood the trials each of them endured, and what it meant to stand before a crowd and speak from the heart on matters of faith. Betray him? Never.

In his room he retrieved his mace and shield and carried them back to Pallos.

"Incredible," said Pallos as Jerico held the shield aloft. The blue-white glow swirled over it, not as strong as it'd been on the night fighting the wolf-men, but nothing he would be ashamed of, either.

"And your mace?" he asked.

Jerico held it closer, so he could see it held no glow, no power. Pallos drew his sword, its blade swirling with the light of Ashhur, showing the strength of his faith.

"When I first heard of this during your training, I didn't believe it," Pallos said, sheathing his sword. "Even coming here, I thought it would have faded over to your mace. Ashhur has granted you a strange gift, Jerico. Never have any of us encountered a paladin's shield becoming his beacon of faith over his weapon. I hope you study it closely to learn its reasons, its limits."

Jerico set the shield down by the tree.

"It's a big hunk of metal that glows. I think I understand it well enough."

Pallos shook his head.

"You should show more reverence to the gifts of Ashhur. The people here study the way you speak, the way you act. You are an example to them, and if you show such callousness toward the miracles of our god, then you will instill them with the same."

Jerico felt his neck flush.

"Yes, sir," he said.

"Come now, I am no teacher, and you no wet-nosed pupil. You are a good man, and I expect greatness out of you. I would not have sent you here if I did not. There are a hundred villages, all needing to hear the word of our god. But Ashhur expects something special from you. I only pray you are prepared for it."

Pallos stood, and he brushed the dirt from his armor.

"I must be going," he said. "There are others who must learn of Mornida's death."

Before he could go, Jerico stopped him.

"Wait," he said. "You see, I…"

"What is it?" Pallos asked.

"I've been having dreams," he said. "The same one, really, and it comes with greater frequency."

The old paladin tilted his head. "Well, tell me, and perhaps I can interpret."

"I see the Citadel. The lower walls are cracking, and then the surrounding field bursts with fire. It's raining, but instead of water, bones fall. I hear a sound, like the roar of a beast, and then I awake."

Pallos looked troubled by what he heard.

"Perhaps you dreamt of Mornida's death," he said. "It is always a troublesome time when our leader falls."

"Are you sure?"

Pallos gestured to the distance. On the other side of the square, Darius was gathering men and women for another sermon.

"Perhaps it is Ashhur warning you of his presence. The Citadel is strong as ever. But to be in the company of a dark paladin…you must expect some of his shadow to fall upon you. Stay safe, Jerico. I hope to see you on my return."

Jerico watched him go as Darius's speech grew louder and filled with fire. He listened for a little while, then went back to the field. More than anything, he wanted the monotony so he might think over what he'd heard, as well as calm the turmoil growing in his breast. It was only an hour later that he realized he'd not once mentioned the wolf-men that had attacked their village.

5

Leaving tower Bronze, Daniel felt an immense sense of relief. Their boat drifted along the center of the river, slow and deep enough they could relax and let the Gihon carry them. Daniel sat in the back, dipping his fingertips in the cold water to keep awake. Not that he needed the help. An argument with someone as stubborn as Sir Lars was easily enough to get him worked up and ready to hit something.

"Unsupplied as I am, you want me to patrol twenty miles south to help protect some...simpletons stupid enough to go into the Wedge?" Lars had asked. He was shorter than Daniel, but still outweighed him by plenty. They'd bickered in his study, him wearing a family breastplate that enhanced his rotund physique.

"At least those simpletons aren't afraid of what they face," Daniel had shot back. Lars had flustered red, and he'd tugged at his long blond mustache while trying to find words to say. During many battles with bandits in the south, as well as the initial skirmishes with the elves, Lars had earned a reputation as a cautious leader. To those with enough alcohol to loosen their tongues, he was a coward, and that cowardice had eventually landed him his position in tower Bronze.

"Sir Godley might be a sour, quiet sod," said one of his men as they drifted along, "but I'd take him any day over that fat weasel Lars."

There were twenty of them, and they all shared a chuckle. The jest was in good nature, but Daniel knew he couldn't let the man get away without reprimand.

"If you've got the energy to waggle your tongue, you can grab some oars and do a bit of rowing, Jon," he said. "I'd hate you to end up as fat as Sir Lars."

More laughs, but they got the point. Jon took to rowing, knowing he'd have to be a fool to try and escape the rather lax punishment. The oars dipped in and out of the water, the sound rhythmic, relaxing. Trees lined either side of them, growing tall with their roots crawling down into the river. Worn stone surrounded both sides, soft rock and dirt half the height of a man. The sun set, the moon rose, but so flat was the river they continued along, two men at the front using poles and lanterns to make sure they had no surprises.

"How far?" asked Jon, a man who had refused to give his last name upon enlistment. Daniel figured him a former bandit or thief, but whatever the crime, he was willing to let it be forgotten so long as he served faithfully, which he did.

"You mean until we're there, or until you stop rowing?" Daniel asked.

"Either's good."

"We should be arriving soon. Keep your eyes peeled for a wooden dock. They should have one, from what I gathered before we left. They rely on a lot of supplies coming up and down the river, given how they're in the middle of nowhere. And put your oars down, Jon."

The man did, and he stretched his back while letting out a pleased grunt.

"Getting shallow," said one of the men with the poles up front. "Might consider pulling off lest we hit something."

"Rather sleep with a roof over my head," Daniel said. "Keep your eyes open and your lanterns west. And hand me one of them, will you?"

Several others joined the search, their shifting rocking the boat enough that Daniel lost the grip of his lantern. It fell to his left, hit the boat, and then rolled off the side. His fingers seemed an inch away the whole while it fell to the water.

"Shit," he muttered, peering off the side. As his eyes lifted, he saw a yellow pair meet his own, then vanish.

"Gregory," he called out, keeping his voice calm.

"Yes, sir?" asked Gregory. He was a young man, but he was strong, and more importantly, had a keen mind. Both Daniel and Robert had wondered how Marcus had erred in letting such a man end up at their towers.

"Look east," he said. "Keep it quiet, and don't make it obvious."

"What am I looking for?" asked Gregory. He put his hands on his back and acted as if he were stretching. The boat continued drifting, many of the men still shining lanterns and searching for the dock, or at the least, distant signs of the village.

"If they're there, you'll know."

Gregory swore. His hand ran through his brown hair, and then it fell to his side, where his sword should have been. It was not. All their gear was stowed in three chests placed equidistant from each other along the center of the boat.

"Eyes watching us," Gregory said.

"How many?"

Daniel leaned his chin in his hand and stared east as if he were bored. Yellow eyes peered at them, and they had a hungry look that sent shivers up his spine.

"At least six pairs. Maybe more. They're wolves, aren't they?"

One of the men near them heard and glanced back, worry crossing his face.

"Wolves, sir?" he asked.

"Shut your mouth, right now," said Daniel. "That's an order."

The man nodded and obeyed.

"What do we do?" asked Gregory, lowering his voice to just above a whisper.

"If there's that many, they aren't here to watch. Can't armor ourselves, otherwise every man tossed overboard drowns."

"I say pass swords around, low and out of sight. And we need to do it fast. I see the eyes no more."

"Have they left?" Daniel asked.

"No," said Gregory, kneeling beside the closest chest and removing the latch. "They went into the water."

"Pull back your lanterns," Daniel ordered his men, and they did so. Gregory started sending swords down the boat, arming the east side first. "Take what we're giving you, and don't act up about it. We got eyes watching us, and Ashhur knows how intelligent they are, and how much they can understand. Jon, Letts, you keep watching for a dock, any dock. Everyone else, scan the river."

Daniel drew his own sword and laid it across his lap, comforted by its weight. If the wolf-men assaulted their boat, there were advantages for either side. The wolves would have surprise, and they'd close the distance without fear of arrows or defensive formations. They'd be slowed by the water, though, and vulnerable trying to climb into the boats. Assuming they tried to climb them, anyway. They were strong, and if they were many, they might be able to overturn their vessel. If that happened, they soldiers would be easy prey.

"Wait for a signal," Gregory said, a sword at his side and a torch in his hand. "A wolf pack won't attack until they get a signal."

The night had gone unnaturally silent. Even the men of the boat were quiet, no longer joking, calling out what they thought might be a deer, stone, or dock. No, they were watching, waiting, cold steel in their hands. Fighting wolf-men without armor, they faced a horrible challenge. Those claws could shred their skin like cloth. Those teeth could rip their limbs from their bodies. Daniel had fought wolf-men plenty in his years guarding the Wedge, but never like this, never ambushed helpless upon the water. And why were they there? The implications were just as frightening as their current situation. To have so many near the Gihon, watching, patrolling even…

From the far bank came the howl, and with that, the water on either side of their boat erupted with claws and teeth. The wolf-men lashed out at them, clawing at the wooden sides and hoisting their bodies upward. With their dark fur wet and matted, they were blacker than the night, just flashes of yellow eyes and eager claws.

Daniel saw two paddling at the rear of the boat, and he lunged with his sword at the first. It lashed up at him, but its paw went wide. His blade slashed its arm, and it yipped in pain, its swimming no longer enough to keep pace. Daniel grinned at the thought of its blood pouring into the river. The second grabbed hold of the rudder, its claws easily sinking in. When Daniel tried to stab it, its teeth snapped back, and startled, he nearly lost his sword.

To his right, a wolf-man lunged high enough to grab the side and pulled itself up. Gregory struck it with his lantern, the light blinding it. His sword pierced its chest, and kicking it off, it fell atop another wolf-man trying to climb in.

"The lantern!" Daniel cried. Gregory tossed it to him. Swearing, Daniel caught it near the bottom, where the heat was greatest. Gritting his teeth to ignore the burning of his hand, he shone its light into the eyes of the wolf-man climbing the back. It snarled, its eyes shut, and then he flung the lantern. The metal struck it in the face, the liquid and fire spilling across its snout. Down it went into the water.

Whirling, Daniel took in the battle before him. The boat rocked unsteadily beneath his feet, both sides buffeted by the many bodies either climbing aboard or falling away. He couldn't count the wolf-men, they were both too many and too hidden. His men were dying. Blood soaked the floor of the boat, mixing with puddles of water. They fought bravely, though, and he felt his heart swell with pride. So far none had panicked, and they stabbed and bled in the darkness like true warriors.

"Beat them back!" he cried, joining Gregory's side. The two slashed at another wolf trying to grab the side, slicing off three claws before it slipped away. With a scream, one of his men went tumbling off the boat, his weak thrust missing, his arm grabbed and pulled. Where he fell became a dark thrashing of water, and then they saw no more. Two more men died, a wolf-man making it into the boat and slashing wildly before soldiers dove upon it, accepting its claws to pierce their blades through its heart. The screams of their pain echoed across the river.

The boat suddenly lurched eastward, accompanied by a deep thunk. Again came a lurch.

"They're guiding us to the Wedge!" someone shouted.

"The poles!" Daniel roared. "Grab the poles!"

They had four poles to push and guide the boat. The first two they plunged into the water snapped as wolf-men grabbed hold of them and bit with their strong teeth.

"Stab the water!" Gregory cried, rushing to the east side and thrusting downward, where several wolf-men had gathered, no longer trying to climb and instead swimming with their heads low and their bodies pushing.

"We hit ground we're dead," Daniel said, grabbing another of the poles. "Now push like your life depends on it!"

The wood groaned in his hand, he heard the yelps of the wolf-men at their side, but at last the pressure relaxed. Once more the boat angled not to the Wedge but instead the opposite side.

"I want off this damn river!" Jon shouted.

"Amen!" cried Daniel.

The last of the wolf-men along the eastern side fell back, the last two poles touching bottom and pushing. Several others grabbed oars, and they rowed toward safety. There was no dock, no landing. They rammed their boat along the rocky shore and then rushed onto dry land with shaky legs.

Exhausted and shivering, Daniel looked out to the river. He saw pairs of eyes watching him from the far side, but not many. It seemed no others gave chase.

"They coming after?" asked Jon.

"Don't look like it," said Daniel. "But we have a long night to go. Get our gear, all of you. Let's put some armor on. If they decide they want to fight, by god, we'll give them one."

While they unloaded the chests, he took count of their losses. Of their original twenty, only eleven remained, counting himself. Nine men, dead or lost along the river. He did his best not to think of it, instead issuing orders and gathering up those who were left.

"How will we find Durham?" asked Gregory, sliding up beside him.

"We'll follow the river south," he said. "Worst comes to worse, and we passed Durham during that mess, we'll eventually reach tower Gold."

"We don't have much food."

Daniel nodded toward a pair of bows his men were unloading from one of their chests.

"We're in the wild now," he said. "We'll hunt if we must."

"While we ourselves are hunted?"

He looked east, those yellow eyes still watching.

"Then we'll see who is the better hunter," Daniel said.

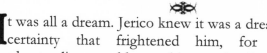

It was all a dream. Jerico knew it was a dream, knew with a certainty that frightened him, for normally that understanding would spur him awake. Instead, the vision continued, with a power and clarity that deepened his fright.

Before him loomed the Citadel, the great tower of Ashhur. Behind it were its docks, and they burned. At its gates he saw a hundred of his brethren. They cried out the name of their god, and their swords shone with the light of their faith. Fighting them were legions of undead. They reached beyond the limits of his vision, for he felt like a raven flying over the battlefield. The undead fell by the scores, but still they came. Jerico's heart soared at his brethren's skill. They would win. Despite the numbers, they would overcome the dead, for they were strong in faith and full of song.

The ground shook, a lion let loose a great roar, and then the Citadel fell.

It crumbled into pieces, its lower foundations breaking at the sides. As it fell, the top half tilted to the right, the heavy dark stone slamming into the ground and tearing free huge chunks of earth. The sound was deafening. Even in his dream he felt his ears ache, and the shockwave of its fall thudded into his chest. The army of paladins below felt it all the more keenly. The light of their weapons, once bright and unshakeable, dwindled. The undead let out a cry, and they charged anew. This time they did not fall so quickly. This time, the paladins did not sing out songs to their god. One by one they fell, until the undead crushed them beneath their feet. Jerico cried out in despair, but he could do nothing, only watch.

He felt an emotion wash over him, and it was not his own. It was a terrible ache, so deep, so overwhelming, that it took him a moment to realize he felt Ashhur's sorrow.

And then he awoke. He lay in his simple bed in his guest room. Sweat covered him. He felt tears in his eyes.

Do not fear the road you must travel, a voice whispered to him. *Only know that you do not travel it alone.*

Alone. The word hit him like a sledge. The vast bulk of his order had died. How many might remain? He thought of the dead he'd seen, and he wondered who commanded them. What nightmare was this? The Citadel, fallen? It'd been prophesied to never fall, for if it did, so would end the order of paladins. And it couldn't end, it couldn't, couldn't...

He felt Ashhur's presence with him, and indeed, believed it was his voice that whispered softly. Deep in his heart, he knew he should feel at peace with such a presence, but he felt only fear and sorrow. His friends. His brothers. His teachers. Dead. So many dead.

Despite all this, he felt a keen sense of exhaustion. He fell back atop his bed, and by the time his head hit the pillow, he was already asleep.

⋈

When Jerico awoke, he remembered the dream, and the passage of time did little to help. As the morning light bathed him, he wished for the images to leave his mind. He'd hoped it would reveal itself a dream, or a possible future to avoid. But all he remembered was a sense of immediacy that denied that hope. He'd felt Ashhur's sorrow. His home was destroyed. The Citadel had fallen.

He heard a knock at the door, then Jessie call out to him.

"Breakfast, if you're ready, sir," she said.

"Thank you," he said, still feeling lost in a dream. He had to get back. He had to see the wreckage for himself, or he might never believe. Besides, who else might be in danger? What of the younger students, had they died in its collapse? And who had led this army? So much he didn't know, didn't understand.

He dressed in his platemail, and he packed his things. Preaching in the village could wait. There were more important things to do.

"Are you leaving us?" Jeremy Hangfield asked as he sat with him at their table.

"I'm afraid I must," he said. Jeremy stared him over, and he felt uncomfortable as he ate.

"You look ill. Is something the matter? A flu, perhaps?"

"Ill," Jerico said, and he shook his head as if his mind couldn't fathom basic conversation. "Ill news from home, perhaps. Thank you, Jeremy. You have been a good host."

"A shame," said Jeremy. "Before you go, Darius wished to speak with you. He said it was urgent, but wouldn't tell me what about."

A strange guilty feeling came over him. Had Darius received a similar dream? How much exaltation would have been in his? Could any paladin of Karak weep for their fall?

"Perhaps I will see him before I go," he said, with no intention of looking.

After excusing himself, he gathered up the rest of his things and hoisted his pack onto his back, over his shield. Jessie was waiting for him at the door.

"Will the Citadel send someone to replace you?" she asked. The question stabbed straight to his heart.

"I fear not," he said.

"I'll miss you. Are you sure you must go? How else will I talk to Ashhur?"

Jerico sighed. She was staring at him from the corner of her eye, as if afraid to meet his gaze. With how haggard and drained he felt, he couldn't blame her. He put his hands on her shoulders and kissed her forehead.

"Even if I go, Ashhur will always remain. Take care, Jessie."

He left their home and trudged south. He'd need supplies later, but he had enough to live on for now. The Citadel had given him plenty of coin, and he'd spent little of it. There would be many villages along the river, and he'd buy what he needed from them. He didn't want to remain in Durham anymore. He felt guilty for abandoning his post, but how could he ignore such a portent sent in his dreams?

Darius spotted him passing through the town square, and inwardly he cursed himself for not going around.

"Jerico!" he said, hurrying over. He wore his armor, and it shone in the light.

"I'm leaving," Jerico said, trying to keep the conversation quick and simple.

Darius looked as if he'd been slapped.

"Leaving?"

Jerico nodded and continued walking. Darius recovered, and he jogged to his side.

"You can't leave," he said. "How could you? The people here need you."

"The wolf-men are dead, and I've done what I can to spread Ashhur's word. Besides, what could you care about that?"

Darius pushed himself into Jerico's way, forcing him to stop.

"Soldiers from Blood Tower arrived several hours before dawn," he said. "They've taken up lodging in several houses, and I've told them not to say anything about what happened."

"What happened? Start making sense, Darius."

"Wolf-men assaulted them upon the river. They lost nine men and had to beach a couple miles outside the village. Right now they're pretending it didn't happen, and they are the full contingent Sir Godley originally sent."

Jerico started to think over the matter, then shook his head and pressed on, his shoulder bumping into Darius's.

"The village is safe enough," he said. "You're here, as are the soldiers now."

"What?" Darius grabbed his arm and pulled him back, forcing him to face him. "I don't know what's going on, but whatever it is, you need to snap out of it. At least twenty wolf-men attacked their boat. They're watching the river, preventing reinforcements. That's not normal, Jerico, and you know it. They're planning an assault. Every single person here is at risk, and I expect a paladin of Ashhur to be brave enough to stand and fight them."

Jerico yanked his arm free and glared.

"You would call me a coward?" he asked.

"I call you nothing. I just wonder what it is that could make you abandon the people who need you most. You said I was wrong to avoid Bobby's funeral, and you were right. Yet now there will be a hundred funerals, assuming any live to bury their dead. Would you be absent from them all? And for what? Tell me what is so damn important!"

Jerico thought of the Citadel's fall, thought of the undead swarming over his brethren. And then he thought of Jessie, sad little Jessie, being shredded by a pack of wolfmen. His clenched fists shook, and he tried to know what was right. In the end, he closed his eyes and asked Ashhur. He received no answer, but in the momentary calm, he felt his guilt overcome him. These people needed him. If Darius was right, and so many were massing along the river…

"I'll stay until the village is safe," he said.

"Good," Darius said, smiling. "Now care to tell me what's the matter?"

Jerico didn't want to imagine the dark paladin's reaction, whether it would be sadness, rejoicing, or indifference.

"Some other time," he said as together they walked back to Durham.

Night of Wolves

6

Daniel ate his breakfast in silence, speaking only to compliment the young woman who had prepared the meal. Amusingly enough, her husband beamed with pride at every word he spoke.

"She's a real cook, ain't she?" said Henry, the husband. His wife, a portly lady with auburn hair, flushed and turned away.

Daniel shifted in his seat. Beside him sat two more of his men, all three having slept on the floor of the farmer's home. Compared to either the boat or the wild, it felt like the softest of beds.

"Never knew oatmeal could taste so fine," said Gregory.

"We may have to stay longer," Jon agreed.

Pushing aside his half-full bowl, Daniel stood. The others fell silent.

"Thank you," he said, tilting his head to the couple. "I have business to discuss, so please, take no offense at my light appetite. The meal was fine, and it is a shame my stomach's not set to enjoy it."

"Want us to come with?" Gregory asked.

"Stay. Rest. I'll talk with the paladins."

The two soldiers shrugged and continued eating.

Daniel shivered as he stepped outside. Pulling his cloak tighter about him, he trudged toward Hangfield's home. Daniel had never met the man, but his name had been on the formal request for aid. That, and when he'd spoken with the paladin Darius upon their arrival, he'd been told to meet them there come the morning.

"You get some rest before we discuss this further," the blue-eyed paladin had told him. Daniel tried to oblige, but his dreams had been full of yellow eyes, and he'd woken multiple times covered with sweat. For all the battles he'd seen, it'd been years since he'd bloodied his blade, and even longer since he'd expected to lose. The feeling was far from welcome.

Damn old age, he thought. What he'd give to have his youthful feeling of invincibility back, if only for a little while.

A pretty lass waited by the door, and she curtseyed to him as he approached.

"Welcome," she said, and he could tell she was trying her best to hide her nervousness.

"Tell me you weren't waiting out here in the chill just for me," he said.

Her gaze fluttered to the ground.

"I was," she said. "Father wishes his guests to feel welcome."

Daniel drew his sword, and her eyes widened. Flipping it about, he stabbed it into the dirt and kneeled before her.

"It is I who should bow to a beauty like you," he said, smiling. "And I who should be waiting in the cold for a greeting. Please gift me with your name."

It warmed his heart to see her giddy and breathless. She was on the cusp of womanhood, and maybe, just maybe, she would remember the honor shown to her and expect similar from the simple men of the village. She reminded him of his own daughter, who he'd lost to the bloody cough so many years before. The girl had the same green eyes. His heart panged at the remembrance.

"Jessie," she said.

"Please, Jessie, escort an old man inside."

She took his offered hand.

"You're hardly old," she insisted. "The hair on your head is not all gray."

"But there is gray in it," Daniel said, opening the door. "And all it takes is a single faded hair to make a man realize how far his youth has fled."

Jessie didn't know what to say, so she quietly led him to the dining room, where both paladins sat, a heavyset man with them.

"Jeremy Hangfield?" he asked as Jessie released his arm.

"I am," said Jeremy. "I trust my daughter was polite in greeting you?"

"Polite as she might be standing motionless in the autumn air." He gestured to a chair. "May I sit?"

Jeremy nodded, ignoring the rebuff. Daniel pulled the chair closer and made a show of sitting down. All the while, he scanned the three men, exaggerating his movements and grunts to buy time. Jeremy had noble blood in him, that was obvious, but he'd been tempered by the farmland and distance from the capital. Having his daughter wait in greeting was just a foolish attempt at replicating distant customs, at pretending to a wealth he didn't really have. He may be the wealthiest man in the village, but compared to the true lords of Mordan, he was insignificant. His house was huge, though, he'd give him that.

The two paladins intrigued him. The one for Ashhur sat to his left, his red hair carefully cut, his beard trimmed.

He wore no armor, but he kept his weapon at his side, and a pendant of the golden mountain hung from his neck. The man looked worn, about as bad as Daniel felt. On the right was Karak's paladin, a handsome man whom he'd met the night before. His blue eyes seemed subdued in the daylight. When they'd first met in starlight, Darius's gaze had sparkled as if infused with sapphires. He also lacked armor, but his greatsword leaned against his chair, his right hand gripping the handle. Compared to the other paladin, he looked a picture of health.

"I suppose introductions are in order," said Daniel.

"I believe you've already met Darius," Jeremy said after dismissing his daughter. He gestured to the other paladin. "And this is Jerico, our guest from the Citadel. Both have done well in protecting our village, but given the threat looming before us, we felt it best to contact you."

"Well, I'm Daniel Coldmine," Daniel said, leaning back in his chair. "I must admit, I first thought your letter a hoax. Wolf-men gathering near the Wedge's border, and even worse, brave enough to cross the river? Preposterous. And to have paladins of both gods unable to stop them, and even more shocking, working together to do so? Now I've heard some tales in my days, gentlemen, but that one nearly got your letter burned."

"We live in strange times," Darius said, chuckling. Jerico remained quiet, and he looked as if his mind were far away.

"Even so, Sir Godley and I decided if it *were* true, things had to be bad indeed. Well, they are, and far beyond it. The wolf-men are scouting the river. They were waiting for us. Waiting! That takes a patience and cunning they normally lack. Whoever leads them is not to be dismissed lightly. They assaulted our boats from the water, killed half my men before we could reach safety. The question we all need to answer is, what does it all mean?"

"Wolf-men have always been territorial," Jeremy said. He drank from his glass, then realized his manners. "A drink, my friend?"

"Strongest you have, Jeremy. I had a long night."

The room fell quiet while Jeremy retrieved him a mug. Daniel scratched at his chin and watched the paladins. Jerico never once met his gaze. Darius seemed bothered by this, and Daniel caught several worried glances directed Jerico's way. So bizarre. The dark paladin was actually upset. Them working together wasn't some diplomatic necessity. They appeared to be friends.

"Strongest ale in the cellar," Jeremy said, sitting back down. Daniel accepted the wooden mug and took a heavy swig. It burned going down, and he loved it. For the first time all morning, he felt himself coming around.

"Thank Ashhur for that. Karak too," he said, winking.

Neither paladin rose to the bait. Damn, they were calm ones, weren't they?

"This isn't territorial," Jerico said suddenly. He looked around, and he had the air of one pulling out of a dream. "They were scouting us with those first attacks. When we crossed the Gihon, they baited us, then attacked from both sides. And now they watch the river, doing all they can to prevent reinforcements. Jeremy, when is the next shipment coming from Bluewater?"

"Their boat should arrive early tomorrow, if not tonight," said Jeremy. "Why?"

"It won't arrive," Darius said, realizing what Jerico was thinking. "The wolf-men will assault it like they did the troops from Blood Tower. They're treating us like an animal separated from its herd."

Daniel frowned. It felt like a bit of a leap, but still...

"Not entirely sure I buy this," he said.

"They've found us weak," Darius said, shaking his head. "And now they'll do whatever they can to starve us, deny us safety in numbers. When will the pack descend upon Durham? And in how great a number?"

"Lot of assumptions here," Jeremy insisted. "We've killed plenty of them. That alone should prove we are no easy prey."

Daniel thought of the viciousness the wolf-men had displayed in attacking their boat. They hadn't cared about their losses or the disadvantages they faced because of the water. No, they'd fought and died to ensure they didn't reach the village. Still, they'd failed, which meant they weren't invincible. Daniel felt pride swell in his chest knowing they'd given as good as they'd gotten, if not better, and that was without armor or solid footing.

"Not easy," Daniel said. He glanced at the three. "But I don't think they expect it to be easy. If they attack here, it will be soon. The longer they wait, the greater the chance Sir Godley realizes the danger and sends more reinforcements from the other towers."

"What is it you suggest?" Jeremy asked.

The paladins shared a look, then deferred to Daniel.

"We either prepare a defense, or flee until we return with greater numbers."

"Fight or flight," said Darius. "It always seems to come down to those two, doesn't it?"

"We cannot leave our homes!" insisted Jeremy. "For nearly everyone here, this is all we have. Our few wagons will not carry a tenth of our possessions. Our livestock will lack for food wherever we go, for how will we bring our grain and hay? Autumn will soon end; there is nothing for us to forage."

"It is better to live with less than die with more," Jerico said.

"Such a fine platitude," Darius said. "But there's a problem. We cannot outrun the wolf-men, not loaded and bearing women and children. Even if we left several days before them, they would descend upon us before we ever reached safety."

"You think their attack will be so soon?" Daniel asked.

"Why else would they attack your ship? Whoever leads them is not stupid. They know time is running out. Even more, I know that defending a caravan of hungry, tired people is far harder than a prepared fortification."

"Prepared fortification?" Jeremy laughed. "We're a farming village. We fish and plant crops. Our homes are plain and made of wood. What fortifications?"

Darius grinned at him, and there was something dangerous in the smile.

"Such little faith," he said.

"Enough," said Jerico. "We don't know what numbers we face. We don't know who leads them and we don't know how much time we have. Everything is guesswork, and in such a state, we are talking out of our behinds. Hot tempers help no one."

"Then what is it you suggest?" Daniel asked, throwing up his hands.

"We go into the Wedge and find out for ourselves."

"We?" asked Jeremy. "Might I remind you how well that turned out last time?"

Darius's face turned red.

"No reminder needed," he said. He glared at Jerico. "And you mean just the two of us, don't you?"

"I do. We slip in and out of the Wedge unnoticed, and when we return, we prepare accordingly."

Daniel stood, feeling the conversation reaching its end.

"And if you do not return?" he asked.

"Then I expect your men to defend this village with their lives," Jerico said, as if it should be obvious. "Whether that is in flight, guarding the river, or behind locked doors, I don't care."

"Of course you don't care," Darius muttered. "We'll be dead, after all."

"These are simple folk," Jeremy said, rising. "Keep news of this to yourselves, all of you. That is the only thing I ask. It's not the unknown they'll fear, only the lack of action. Once we know what we're to do, trust me, trust us, to stand tall and do what must be done."

Daniel turned to leave, and as he did, he heard Darius's biting comment behind him.

"Very few stand tall when staring into the eyes of a wolf-man, Jeremy. Pray we return with good news."

❖

Redclaw's fury swelled as Yellowscar groveled before him, his belly pressed against the pale grass and his snout jammed into the ground. Every quaking breath blew dirt back and forth from his nostrils. Across his arm was a shallow wound, the blood crusted over and matting his fur.

"Twice now you fail me," Redclaw said. The rest of the pack surrounded him, for when Yellowscar's group had returned, they'd come limping with wounds and half their original number. The pack had sensed blood then, and come to watch it drawn. Redclaw keenly felt their eyes upon him, and his law of wolf not killing wolf weighed heavily on his shoulders.

"I have earned your wrath, pack leader," Yellowscar said. "They were prepared somehow, and when we burst from the water, they struck us with swords and pushed toward the shore with heavy poles."

Again the numbers confounded Redclaw. He'd sent twenty-five wolf-men to deal with what turned out to be a mere twenty humans. Nine humans had died, to fourteen wolves. How could such a thing happen? Was he underestimating their weak, pink flesh? The orcs wielded weapons akin to the humans, yet they died in droves when they descended upon them. What made these humans so much more dangerous?

They couldn't be. The failure came in the leader, the commander.

"Yellowscar," Redclaw said, grabbing him by the neck and lifting him from the ground. "I see now where the fault lies."

And with that, he pressed his nose against Yellowscar's, a sign of friendship and forgiveness. All around, the pack yipped and growled with confusion.

"I have sent scouts to do the job of warriors. I have sent the fast do the work of the strong. It is I who should have led this charge, to witness for myself the strength of humans. They were brave enough to come into the Wedge and slay many of my pack. Vengeance, my brethren! That is what we must howl for."

He narrowed his eyes and lowered his voice.

"You will sleep outside the pack for the rest of your life," he growled. "Twice now you fail me, and yet I humble myself so you may live. Wolf must not slay wolf. But twenty wolves died under your lead, yet you did not. So that is how many you must slay before I accept you back into our warmth."

"My mate..."

"You may not lie with her, nor cuddle with your pups. They stay with us, and you outside. Do you understand, Yellowscar, or must I name you Yellowbelly to the entire pack?"

Yellowscar flattened his ears and lowered his head.

"I understand. I will earn my way back with blood, pack leader. I promise."

Redclaw stepped back and looked west.

"Time has become our enemy. Let us go to the river. Another boat should arrive, this of food and tools, yes?"

"Every seven days, and tonight is the seventh," Yellowscar said, looking pleased that his watch was proving useful in any way.

"Good. Let us see if you can feast upon the first of your twenty."

Redclaw gathered fifteen of his strongest, including Yellowscar, and then ran toward the water. The ugly grass grew thicker, some of its color turning to traces of healthy green. The moon was bright in the sky, and Redclaw felt pleasure in its light. It was a cool presence, soft on his eyes, unlike the fiery day. With everything so bright, it seemed the world shimmered, the colors flushed and exaggerated. In the darkness, his eyes soaked in the curves of the grass, the drifting of the clouds, and the jutted crevices of each stone, all without long distorting shadows. Up ahead, trees grew, a sign they had arrived at the river the humans called the Gihon.

"Why did you not bring Bonebite?" asked Yellowscar as they slowed, walking on their hind legs instead of all fours.

"Why? Do you feel fright without him to cower behind?" snapped one of the other warriors, brown-furred and wide-shouldered with the name of Dirtyhide. Redclaw shot him a glare, and he nipped at his face to show his displeasure.

"It is no cowardice to want a strong warrior at your side," he snarled. "Calm yourselves, all of you. This is Yellowscar's hunt."

"A doomed hunt then," Dirtyhide grumbled.

Redclaw bared his teeth, and before the other wolf could respond, he grabbed him by the throat and lifted his back legs off the ground.

"I fight at his side," he said. "You insult *me* in saying us doomed. Speak it again, Dirtyhide, if you are so brave. I relish the thought of your blood on my tongue."

"Wolf must not kill wolf," Dirtyhide managed to say, his clawed fists clutching Redclaw's wrist as it held him.

"I would only eat one arm. You'd still live."

Dirtyhide yipped at that. Giving him one last shake, Redclaw tossed him to the ground and snarled at the others. He towered a foot above all of them, and he pulled back and howled to the moon, letting them hear the strength of his lungs, see the corded muscles of his chest. The rest backed away, all but Yellowscar, who lowered his head and ears respectfully while staying at his side.

"Enough," said Redclaw. "We must not nip at our own heels when food is near. To the river. The human village must starve as we starve. They must know the hunger we have lived with all our lives. No boats can arrive. As for Bonebite, he remains at the pack for I need him at the Gathering. I would not want Goldteeth to arrive without someone strong to greet him."

"We don't need Goldteeth to feast upon the human flesh," said Rockeye, looking to the rest for support. He was stronger than many, his powerful muscles visible through the mange on his skin, but it was for his reflexes that Redclaw brought him. "Send Goldteeth away. Let his pack starve while we reap what we have earned."

"I said enough!" Redclaw snarled. "You are my strongest, yet you doubt me? We do not attack to eat. We attack to live! The humans will send men to drive us back across the river, hundreds of them. With our every victory, more will arrive, until we face a sea of metal and flesh. Come then, we must have every wolf-man united together. I cannot be just pack leader. I must be leader of leaders. Humans are fearful of the future, and that is why they will never let us be. We must be smarter. We must be stronger. Goldteeth will only be the first."

"You are strong," Yellowscar said, still keeping his body low. "Not since the old tales have we had a leader of leaders, but you are mighty. You will be Wolf King."

The rest howled at the title, and Redclaw felt a shiver crawl up his spine.

"Wolf King," he said, drool swelling on his tongue. "If the moon is kind, I will see it so. But for now, the boat. Let us worry about Goldteeth and his pack later. Ears sharp, and noses open. They must not pass."

They fell silent, the only sound that of their footfalls and the deep inhalations through their nostrils. The world was awash with colors, not just of light, but of scent. They floated like mists before him, should he let his mind focus upon the sense. When on the hunt, the mist would trail through the air, fading with each moment, falling upon the grass and leaves like dew. But his eyes were sharp, his nose strong, and he could smell what others could not, track what others could not. And in the night, hovering like smoke across the water, was the scent of humans.

"Already passed here," Redclaw growled.

"Not long," said Yellowscar, whose nose was stronger than his, which is why he was a scout. "The scent is heavy. Let us run. No boat along the water can match the speed of a wolf."

"Send them our fear," Redclaw said, taking in a deep breath as the others did likewise. As one they howled, the sound traveling for miles. He wished he were close enough to smell the human's fear on the boat. Surely it would be delicious.

South along the river they ran. They moved without need for silence. This territory had long been theirs, and there was no creature that would dare hunt a wolf-man. The river curved, gently widening. The trees grew taller and further apart. As Redclaw ran, he kept his concentration off the scent. It was just a vague swarm of color to him, and unless he slowed down he could make no sense of it. Yellowscar, however, yipped and pointed, able to decipher meaning even when at full run.

"Very close," he said. "But the town is close as well. Hurry."

"It is your hunt," Redclaw told him. "Lead on, and show no hesitation."

They thundered along, Yellowscar leading, Redclaw following with the rest of his hunting party. The trees were a blur as they passed by. Panting heavily, Redclaw watched the moon steadily dip. Morning would arrive all too soon, along with the damned fire in the sky. He wondered how Bonebite handled himself at the Gathering. They greatly outnumbered Goldteeth's pack, but with him and his greatest warriors gone, the other leader would grow bold, as he hoped. Still, that was for another time. The hunt was on, and he couldn't risk distraction.

He didn't need Yellowscar's signal to know the boat was near, for between the trees his sharp eyes spotted the humans. There were six, sitting on a large, flat structure that floated along. Several crates were stacked atop it. Whether or not the humans wielded metal weapons, he didn't know. They often hid them in strips of leather at their sides, and with them sitting, he could not see.

"Howl or swim?" Yellowscar asked, keeping his voice low.

"Your hunt," Redclaw said.

Yellowscar continued his run, and faster than the river they continued south. Soon the boat was behind them, and then Yellowscar sprinted into the water. Redclaw followed, and he did his best to hide his discomfort. There were many of his brethren who loved to paddle in the water. They claimed it made them feel free, but Redclaw always felt trapped. It made him slower, his claw strikes weak and clumsy. Before his pack, though, he couldn't dare show weakness. He remained at Yellowscar's left, only their heads visible above the water as they paddled.

"No deaths," Redclaw whispered. Yellowscar flattened his ears in response.

The six men were clearly on edge. It mixed with their scent, changing its color. Two rowed, and a third guided them along with a heavy pole. Three more sat in the center, and it was they that Redclaw assumed would have weapons. Yellowscar snapped his teeth to the left, then to the right. The pack split, half one way, half the other. Redclaw led the left. Only Yellowscar remained at the front, and he stopped his paddling. The boat drifted toward them, moving faster than the river.

Redclaw shifted closer, checking his positioning. By the time they reached Yellowscar, he would be within grabbing distance of an oarsman. The other side would be similarly attacked, and Yellowscar could surely handle the man with the pole. Half the boat would be bleeding in the water before they knew they were under attack. He felt his anticipation rise, saliva building on his tongue. Closer, closer...

He was just about to reach out when Yellowscar burst from the water and howled at the top of his lungs. The oarsmen jerked back, and Redclaw's swipe missed. Furious, he paddled closer to the boat as the humans cried out in panic. The boat was a confusion of bodies and arms. Snarling, Redclaw grabbed the side and hoisted himself up. The man with the oar had dropped it to grab a blade, and he swung it with strength born of desperation. With no room to move, and no desire to fall back into the water, Redclaw endured the slash. It tore into his flesh, but his muscles were thick, and his hide tough. Blood spilled across his fur. He slashed the oarsman, trading him blow for blow. The human had only weak skin, and beneath his sharp claws, it shredded and tore. An eyeball flung loose from the human's skull, and Redclaw felt disappointment as it plopped into the water, sure to be lost and eaten by fish.

His fury growing, he lunged at the men in the center, the three of them keeping their backs together and their swords thrusting. They wore light armor, like the scales of fish, and his claws caught and pulled. One went down, the blow surely breaking bones. Another tried slashing at him to protect his comrade, but two wolf-men attacked from the other side. Just like that, the defense collapsed. More and more of his pack climbed aboard, tossing bodies into the water so the rest could feast.

At last they were dead, and Redclaw stood in the boat's center. The blood-haze faded from his mind, and once more he took in his surroundings. The village's dock was within sight.

Grabbing a crate, he hefted it into his arms and dumped it into the river. The rest followed his example, filling the river with old meats, filthy grains, and blocks of salt. Finished, he looked about, and when he saw the body floating face down, his fury swelled anew.

"Dirtyhide," he said. His voice was calm, belying his fury. He searched for Yellowscar, found him at the back of the boat, his mouth hanging open with a dumb expression. Redclaw let loose a howl and leapt at him. His claws tore two great stripes across Yellowscar's chest, soaking his claws with blood. Yellowscar moved to defend himself, but Redclaw grabbed his throat and squeezed. Knowing struggling was useless, Yellowscar lay there, the thin layer of water along the bottom of the boat soaking into his fur.

"You gave us away!" he cried.

"I wanted them afraid," Yellowscar argued.

"And I wanted them dead! Dirtyhide died. I warned you, Yellowscar. Three times is your failure, and how many did you kill this night?"

"Two."

"Two? You are pathetic. You are weak."

He picked him up and hurled him into the water. When he tried to come near, the others nipped at him and chased him away.

"The territory of Redclaw is no longer your home," he decreed. "Step one foot in my land, and we will cut you, bleed you, and leave you for the vultures. Do you understand me, Yellowscar?"

Yellowscar ignored them, instead paddling toward the human side of the river. When he reached the shore, he turned back and howled.

"I will come for my pups. I will come for my mate. You will not banish me, Redclaw!"

"You *are* banished, Yellowscar! And I will take your mate as my own, for her fur is soft, and she deserves a stronger mate than you."

Yellowscar howled again, this one mixed with anger and helpless anguish. Redclaw responded in kind, and his cry was louder, stronger, and it humbled the banished wolf-man.

"Come," he told his brethren. "We shall return home. The humans will suffer now, and they will worry. Let us see how the Gathering has gone, and if Bonebite has earned us another ally."

They swam west, back into the Wedge. Redclaw looked back only once, curious to see if a pair of yellow eyes watched them from the opposite shore. There were none. Yellowscar was gone.

Night of Wolves

7

"Careful with the boat," Jerico said as Darius guided them across the Gihon. "I doubt either of us could do much swimming in platemail if you capsize us."

"I can remove my armor in less than twenty seconds. Can you?"

"A handy skill with the ladies, I guess."

Darius shot him a wink. "I didn't think that would be something a paladin of Ashhur would know much about."

Jerico laughed. "Just watch the river. I doubt any comely lasses are waiting for you at the bottom."

They stowed the boat amid the tall reeds growing by the river's edge. From there they checked their armor, tightened it, and began their trek.

"Keep that shield on your back," Darius said as they jogged. "Last thing we need is your glow giving us away."

"Perhaps you should have ducked into the river. I wonder which is noticeable from farther away, my shield's light, or your smell?"

"Your insults are like those of children."

"Didn't you tell me I should adept to my audience?"

Darius hit him with an elbow, which clanged against his platemail. Jerico grinned and smacked his shoulder. For a long while they ran, the minutes passing by in relative silence. The river faded behind them, soon just a barely visible line of trees. At last they stopped for a breather, and Jerico wondered at how many miles they had crossed.

"I think I know why elves only wear leather," Jerico muttered as he tugged at the undercoat of his armor.

"We're slower to arrive, and slower to be killed," Darius said. "Fair tradeoff."

"From what I hear, they're tough to kill as well."

Darius shrugged. "Well, they'd be even harder to kill in plate. Must you always debate?"

"Must you always be right?"

"It's my charming trait. What's yours?"

"The red beard."

Despite the heaviness of his breath, Darius laughed.

"Fair enough. I see no wolf tracks here, and the night is strangely void of their howls."

Jerico shifted the shield on his back and then gazed west, which was a long stretch of flat ground leading to where hills grew like bumps atop the wedge. In the starlight, he saw only grass and rock.

"It is strange," he agreed. "Did we pass their camp, perhaps?"

"I doubt that. They run faster and farther than us, so it'd make sense for them to keep distance between their pack and the river. Last thing they want is easy surprise by our soldiers. But still, why the silence? Surely there's at least one pack out there hunting."

"What if they're hunting us?"

They both glanced about, and Jerico felt the hairs on his neck rise.

"Your god warning you of impending danger?" Darius asked.

"No. You?"

"No. Then we're not being hunted...yet. Come. In time, the wolf-men will have to..."

The cacophony of howls stunned him quiet. It came from their north, the wild sounds crying to the moon. Their volume was so great both paladins shivered, their mouths dropping open in surprise.

"It can't be," Darius whispered.

"We have to see for certain," Jerico said, swallowing his fear.

"But there are hundreds. Hundreds!"

"And we will get as close as we can to know for sure." Jerico struck Darius across the chest with the back of his hand, an almost playful gesture. "You aren't losing your spine on me, are you?"

A second wave of howls reached them, accompanied by many faster yips. Darius listened, then shook his head as if snapping out of a daze.

"Spine is still intact," he said, staring hard to the north. "But we won't be if any spot us. They'll devour even our bones, Jerico. Lead on if you must. No paladin of Ashhur will go where a paladin of Karak will not."

Jerico took point, almost wishing Darius had objected more strongly. Part of him wanted to get as far away from that fearful gathering as possible. From what he could tell, they were somewhere between the dips of the hills, but where, he did not know. Sound could do strange things when traveling across the plains. The two ran on, their idle chatter ended, their breathing muffled. The rattle of their armor suddenly seemed dangerous and unnecessary. Leather armor, thought Jerico. Yet another reason to wear that instead of this damn plate.

They slowed as they approached a tall hill, and from the other side they heard constant shouts and growls. The wolf-men spoke the tongue of humans, as all creatures other than the orcs of the Wedge did. Ever since their creation and subsequent use in the Gods' War, the wolves had changed it the least, while the other races had added strange accents to fit their tongues. Jerico remembered studying each race during his time in the Citadel, and now he wished he'd paid ten times more attention to those studies. What could the wolf-men possibly be doing raising such a ruckus?

"Stay low," Darius said as they neared the hill. "The wind favors us, so thank Karak for that."

"Karak's lord of the air?"

"And the dirt. Now shut up and follow me."

Darius climbed on his hands and knees, and Jerico followed. Near the very top they began crawling on their stomachs, and at the summit, they peered over to witness the gathering of wolf-men. Jerico's jaw dropped at the number. There were at least two hundred, and they formed a great circle around a massive pile of rock that, he guessed, was sacred to them in some way. At first he thought them one group, but then he saw they were sectioned into two. On the left was the larger, nearly a hundred and fifty, while on the right was a group a third that size.

"Their leaders," Darius whispered as he pointed. Jerico followed his gaze. Two wolf-men stood beside the rock pile, and they took turns howling. One of them, representing the larger group, had gray fur and a heavy stoop to its back, but its size and strength was incredible. The other, taller but thinner in the arms, snarled and consistently bared its ugly yellow teeth. Whatever they said between their howls, neither paladin could hear through the din.

"We've seen enough," Darius said.

"Wait." Jerico grabbed his arm and then gestured. "Something's going on."

The two leaders stepped onto the pile of rocks. They scattered and shifted, and then Jerico realized they were no rocks. They were bones, an enormous collection, all of them incredibly old. With their ascension, the rest quieted so they might hear their leaders speak.

"I am Bonebite," said the older wolf-man. "I speak for Redclaw, pack leader of his tribe. Let all look upon me and know my strength."

Bonebite stood to his full height and howled. It went on and on, at a pitch that made Jerico's ears ache.

"I am Goldteeth," said the other. "Pack leader of my tribe. Let all look upon me and know my strength."

Goldteeth's turn to howl, and this time Jerico plugged his ears with his fingers. His howl was louder, but did not last as long. He wondered which one would be considered the greater. Was that a lecture he slept through at the Citadel? Maybe he could take his knowledge back to his teachers and...

He felt a pain in his chest as he remembered his vision of the Citadel's collapse. No, there would be no teachers, no students, no lessons. Biting his tongue to focus, as well as fight back tears, he listened as the wolf-men resumed whatever strange ritual they'd stumbled upon.

"You called us here," Goldteeth said, his howl still ringing in Jerico's ears. "We come to the Gathering. Why is Redclaw not here? Must he hide behind others? Must he use your strength, Bonebite?"

The larger group growled, the sound low and deep.

"Redclaw hides behind no one," said Bonebite. "His pack is strong, and he is stronger than I. Would you insult what you cannot strike, Goldteeth?"

The other's turn to growl and yip. Jerico strained his eyes to see. Goldteeth had bared his fangs, and he paced before Bonebite. His fingers opened and closed, as if he were imagining burying his claws into a foe.

"I hear his reason, and I come now to challenge it. Redclaw would seek to be leader of leaders, yet he will not appear at his own Gathering? I will not bow my head to such a coward. Hear me, it is I that should lead your pack. Goldteeth is the stronger, and Redclaw the weakling."

"Then why is your pack the smaller?" asked Bonebite. He gestured toward them, as if mocking their numbers. "If you are stronger, why does your pack not rival ours?"

"You grow fat on better land," argued Goldteeth. "You hunt by the river in your secret place, but it is secret no longer. We also hear of the weakness of Redclaw. My pack is small, but it is strong. You nurse weaklings and gray-furs. You do not cull the lesser. Two wolves can destroy twenty cows, Bonebite the gray-fur."

"That got under his skin," Darius muttered as Bonebite howled at the top of his lungs, the rest of his pack joining in.

"Still not sure what we're watching," Jerico said, raising his voice to be heard.

"A pissing contest is my guess. I also think Bonebite's pack is the one that's been giving us trouble."

Jerico agreed, and he quieted down as the events unfolded. The two leaders were crouching before one another on the pile of bones, their teeth bared and their ears flattened.

"I challenge you!" Bonebite howled, and the rest of his pack nearly lost themselves in their excitement.

"You fight for Redclaw!" Goldteeth shot back. "He must accept my victory."

"You will have no victory," Bonebite snarled.

"Swear it!"

"Redclaw will accept!" cried Bonebite. "But you will fall to this gray-fur, you proud, stupid pup."

"Holy shit," Darius said, his mouth dropping open. The two wolf-men lunged with vicious speed, slashing their claws into each other's flesh. Their teeth snapped and bit, and the blood quickly flowed. Jerico watched best he could, considering the distance and the darkness. He imagined himself fighting either, and the results didn't seem promising. They were towering figures of muscle and fur, teeth and claw. Based on Darius's cursing and slack jaw, Jerico could tell he felt the same.

At first, Goldteeth seemed to hold the advantage. He tore into Bonebite, his claws raking along his opponent's shoulders. Several times he stopped to ram him, pushing Bonebite toward the edge of the bones.

"They must stay atop it," Jerico said, suddenly realizing the match's sole rule. "That's how they'll decide."

Bonebite went defensive as his back feet pressed against the final pieces of bone. His head dipped low, and his broad shoulders curled inward, his elbows pressed tight to his sides so his hands might protect his face. The other members of the packs howled and cheered, depending on whose side they rooted for. To Jerico, it almost seemed like they cheered for the sight of blood no matter who spilled it. Goldteeth slashed at Bonebite, who swayed with the blows, preventing them from gaining any strength. Blood dripped down his arms from the shallow cuts. When Goldteeth bit, Bonebite's claws were there, pushing him back and always threatening to hook his snout.

Losing his patience, Goldteeth suddenly lunged, all his weight bearing down on his opponent. Jerico tensed, expecting the confrontation to end, but the older wolf-man was a cunning one. Instead of trying to block the blow, or step out of the way, he stood erect and opened his arms wide. Goldteeth barreled into him, quickly wrapped in Bonebite's iron grip. Bonebite spun, slamming Goldteeth to the bones beneath him. The two snapped at one another, but Bonebite had leverage, and his teeth sank into the vulnerable flesh of Goldteeth's neck. The horde of wolf-men cried louder. Blood spurted across the bones.

Goldteeth was too strong to die from a single bite, though. He forced a roll, his back feet kicking and slashing wounds into Bonebite's thighs. The two came to a stand, facing one another for a brief second. They were both badly wounded, Goldteeth seeping blood from his neck, Bonebite from the many slashes along his arms and legs. They exchanged a few swipes, but Bonebite was the faster, and his claws found flesh.

And then Bonebite dove in, with such ferocity that Jerico found himself unprepared. The wolf-man's claws slashed and grabbed, his teeth rent flesh, and in an explosion of gore he tore Goldteeth apart. Even those of Goldteeth's tribe cheered, showing just how deeply their loyalty ran for their leader.

Bonebite lifted Goldteeth's heart to the moon, and as he did, the crowd quieted.

"You of Goldteeth's pack, do not swear to me as you might have once done. You will remain a pack, separate from us, but still strong, still loyal. Find yourselves a new leader, and he will swear loyalty to Redclaw. Redclaw will be the leader of leaders! Redclaw will be the moon made flesh. Redclaw will be Wolf King!"

"This is bad," Jerico said, his throat dry. Darius nodded in solemn agreement.

"It's time we leave, now."

Wolves from Goldteeth's former pack were climbing onto the pile of bones, no doubt to battle over who would become the new leader. Jerico watched for only a moment, then turned to follow Darius back to their boat. A single frightening thought hammered his mind repeatedly: whoever this Redclaw was, Bonebite considered him stronger. How fearsome must he be in battle, for Bonebite alone looked like he could tear apart ten armored soldiers.

Halfway to the river, Darius suddenly grabbed him and flung him to the ground.

"Quiet," he hissed, but the order was unnecessary. Jerico felt Ashhur crying warning in his head, and it pounded like a drum. They lay in the tall grass, the silence of the night all around them. And then, a hundred yards to the north, ran the wolf pack. Jerico could not count them all, but there were at least ten, if not twenty. It was their leader that held his eye, and he watched as long as he could before they vanished. The wolf-man was enormous, towering over the others even when he ran on all fours.

"We're downwind," Darius whispered when they were finally gone. "Thank Karak for that."

"Ashhur as well," Jerico said, standing. He stared in the distance, a chill running up his spine. "Where did they come from, Darius? What is it they have done?"

They found their answer at the river. Beached not far from their boat was another, this one wide and flat. When they searched it, they found no trace of the supplies that had surely been atop it, and as for the men who piloted it, they found only their blood. The river, or the bellies of the wolves, had claimed the rest. Jerico whispered prayers for the fallen men while Darius cursed and turned his gaze east.

"You were right," said the dark paladin. "They'll starve and weaken us, and still they watch the river. Whoever this...Redclaw is, his pack is growing. When will they attack? When will they swim over these waters and tear this village apart?"

"I don't know," Jerico said, finishing his prayer. "But they will. Of that, I have no doubt."

"Come then," Darius said, heading toward their boat. "Let us share the bad news. Tomorrow morning, they're leaving, all of them. We cannot defeat such a force on our own."

"What if they catch us while we flee?"

Darius laughed and reached out his hand to help Jerico into the boat.

"Then I guess we'll have to win anyway. What's wrong, paladin, lost your faith in the impossible? Hopefully not yet. We've still got to convince a couple hundred farmers and wives to leave everything they have based on the testimony of two men."

"They'll listen," Jerico insisted.

"We'll see," Darius said, and they let the subject die.

Redclaw detected the scent of his many brethren within the hills, and it warmed his heart. His two pups, still without names since they were yet to reach their first year, would be there among them. Hopefully one of his pack members had ensured them a close seat for when Bonebite challenged Goldteeth. They should witness such strength firsthand, see what it meant to face a rival and conquer him without hesitation or remorse.

The rest of his party loped behind him, and Redclaw did his best to put Yellowscar out of his mind. The fool had endangered his pack, cost him the life of a fine warrior, and revealed himself lacking in any sense of cunning or tactic. Let the humans kill him once he grew fat on the plentiful game waiting across the great river.

"Do you think Goldteeth won?" Rockeye asked.

"Goldteeth is stupid. His pack is small because even the wild dogs think better. He will expect to win on strength alone. Bonebite is smart. Bonebite is fast. I have no doubt who won. Goldteeth's pack will swear their allegiance to me."

They crossed the hills, and as they did, something tugged at the back of Redclaw's mind, like a thorn that had worked its way underneath his skin. Ignoring it, he slowed his run so he might arrive standing tall and proud instead of with his tongue hanging out the side of his mouth. As they walked, Rockeye cocked his head and listened.

"The Gathering nears its end," he said. "I hear them howling in celebration."

"A new leader," Redclaw said. "Let us meet him."

They entered the circle, and Redclaw was pleased to see the sacred mound soaked in blood and gore. The best Gatherings were ones where not a shred of bone remained white come the rise of day. Three dead wolf-men lay atop it, with one lone survivor standing, his left eye swollen shut and the fur of his chest hanging ragged from torn skin.

"Bring him to me," Redclaw said as Bonebite came closer.

"Of course," said Bonebite. The dead wolf-men were placed before their pack, and they began their feast. Redclaw looked for his pups while he waited. Sure enough, they were near the front, within easy view of the bone mound. He grinned, and when they saw him, they respectfully dipped their heads. Pleased, he looked to the new pack leader, who came and knelt before Redclaw.

"I am Moonclaw," said the wolf. "My pack swears its loyalty to you, mighty Redclaw. Bonebite fought in your stead, and his tongue tasted much blood. We will learn from that strength."

Redclaw narrowed his eyes as he looked over the new pack leader. He had an almost lanky appearance, for while he was as tall as Redclaw, he lacked the muscle. His fur was a deep black, with a few splotches of white across his face and hands.

"I must see you fight another time," Redclaw said. "I wish to judge your strength, but tonight, I deem you leader of your pack."

"And I deem you leader of leaders, Wolf King."

Moonclaw bowed even lower, and Redclaw felt his heart leap at the title. So it had begun, small perhaps, only the tiny step of a pup, but a step nonetheless. The wind shifted, swirling for a brief moment, and with it color poured over the hills south, the scent faint but inescapably human. Redclaw felt panic only a moment, swiftly replaced by anger.

"They were here!" he roared. "Humans! They watched the Gathering, and none of you saw? None of you heard their whispers, smelled their scent?"

"The noise was great," said Moonclaw. "And what else could we smell but the blood upon the mound?"

"Forgive us," Bonebite said, stepping back and lowering his head. "I heard and smelled nothing either. The wind was their ally, and the noise of the Gathering their friend."

Redclaw let loose a rumble from deep within his belly. The rest of his pack gathered around him, remaining just far enough back to maintain a respectful distance. He felt his plan weaving through his head. They lacked the numbers for what he desired. They could slaughter the village, that he knew, but it was the humans that would come from afar that he feared. So far he'd kept his numbers hidden from them, but if any had seen the Gathering, had seen the force building so very near…

"Moonclaw, Bonebite, with me," he said. "We have much work to do, even beneath the angry fire of the sky. Rockeye, go west to the packs of Bloodfang and

Murdertongue. Summon them to a Gathering. We have little time."

"Yes, Wolf King," said Rockeye, leaving at once. Redclaw walked south, the two strong wolf-men following him. He found where the men had lain, and he inhaled their scent. There had been a pair of them, and they stayed for a long while. Shaking his head, he turned to Bonebite and Moonclaw.

"No help," he said. "No rescue. No chance for war. Hear my plan, Moonclaw. Hear me, Bonebite. Our freedom from the Wedge begins at dawn."

Night of Wolves

8

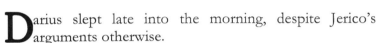

Darius slept late into the morning, despite Jerico's arguments otherwise.

"Either the wolf-men will catch us, or they won't," he'd said. "I don't think me getting a few hours of sleep will matter one way or the other."

"The people of Durham need to prepare."

"Then you wake at dawn and tell them," Darius had said as he set aside his armor and slipped into bed. "Meanwhile, the sky's still dark and my head feels like two wolf-men are fighting inside. Good night."

His head felt little better come waking, but at least it had lost some of its knife edge of pain. His legs ached from the many miles they'd walked, and his back was sore for doing it all while wearing his armor. He stayed in the sole upper room of Durham's inn, and he came down to have breakfast with the lady of the place, a widow named Dolores.

"Bread and honey as always?" he asked her, trying for levity.

"You'll make do with porridge," she said, not a smile on her wrinkled face. "The whole town's talking, and it's got me scared. I can't leave everything behind, Darius."

Even riding in a cart will make my old bones groan, and what hope could I have to earn a living elsewhere?"

"I hear a beautiful woman such as yourself earn quite a lot in the back alleys of Mordeina."

She slapped his head with a rag, and he grinned at her. Seemed like Jerico had already met with Jeremy, and he felt relieved. Let him deal with that enormous hassle. He began eating his meal.

"Oh, dear me, slipped my mind," Dolores said a few minutes later. "A man came to speak with you, but I told him you'd been out at night helping us and you don't take kindly to waking up early. He said he was one of you, at least in a way. A priest, he said. I offered him a room, but he said he wouldn't be staying long."

"A priest?" Darius asked. "Where is he now?"

"Said for you to meet him at the square. He seemed in quite a hurry."

"Thank you, Dolores. I'd best be going then."

He hurried back up the stairs, trying to make sense of things. Sometime in the next few months he knew a paladin of Karak was supposed to check in on his progress, but a priest? Had he just happened to pass by Durham? Or were they to change his assignment? Priests were considered superior to paladins in Karak's hierarchy, and if the priest gave him an order, he would have no choice but to obey. Still, his arrival was certainly fortuitous in other ways. Perhaps he might help with the wolf-men, or know of a better plan than simply tucking their tails between their legs and running.

Once he was dressed in his armor, his sword sheathed on his back, he came down.

"Did he say a name?" he asked Dolores before stepping outside.

"I reckon he did," said the woman. She tapped her teeth with a fingernail. "Slipped my mind, though. Seemed polite enough, though I wouldn't wish him around long. Got a queer air about him. Cold, too."

"Thanks."

Darius pushed open the door and hurried his way to the square. Jerico found him first. A mob of seven or eight surrounded him, and he pushed his way toward the dark paladin.

"Enjoy your nap?" Jerico asked.

"Tremendously," Darius said, forcing a grin. "Enjoy your talk with Jeremy?"

"He saw reason, thank Ashhur. The whole town will be heading south. We're fifteen miles from Wetholm, and I doubt the little village can manage to feed even a third of us, but it's better than nothing. We'll just have to make do."

"Sure thing," Darius said, his eyes looking past him. Jerico evidently noticed, and he frowned.

"Something the matter?" he asked.

"No. Yes. Just a friend."

Jerico glanced behind, and a bit of his cheer vanished.

"He's been here all morning. I've stayed away out of respect. Any help the priests and paladins of Karak can offer would be appreciated."

The group returned, asking Jerico questions and requesting aid.

"Will you be helping everyone prepare?" Darius asked before he turned away.

"We leave after midday. Not much time, so we'll be stretched thin. Help who you can, and I'll do the same."

"As you say." Darius pushed past him, toward the lone tree growing near the square. Leaning against it, being given a wide berth by the rest of the town, was a man in the black robes of a priest. His head was shaved, and a multitude of pendants made of silver and iron hung from his neck. He stood straight, his thin shoulders pulled back. His blue eyes lacked any amusement as Darius came before him and kneeled.

"Welcome to Durham, brother," he said, his head low. "I hope your travels have been safe."

"Nothing in this world is safe," said the priest. He glanced at Jerico, and his frown deepened. "Least of all here. I come with great tidings, though I wish my heart would not be so troubled when I tell you. Do you remember me, Darius? I was there when you were first assigned along the river."

Darius remembered, two years prior at the gates of the Stronghold. He'd completed the Trials, and having come of age, they gave him his first assignment: to travel along the northern stretches of the Gihon, preaching to the many villages that had gone years without hearing Karak's word. The ceremony had been solemn, and his heart swelled with pride. Two priests had attended, invited to the special event. One had remained quiet, but the other...his eyes had the same icy blue, and his words still stung.

You are young, full of faith, and yet in you I sense a chaos rumbling. Mind your heart, your thoughts, and your ideas. Among the simple folk you belong, for I fear your reaction should you face a true challenge of Ashhur.

"Yes," he said. "I remember you now, though I was never given your name."

"I am Pheus, and it seems I was correct. How long has the paladin of the false god preached in your village, Darius?"

Darius felt his face flush.

"Perhaps a year, at most."

"You have not driven him out? You have not rallied the villagers against him? Worse, I see you speaking with him. Have you reached some agreement with this paladin, some sort of truce? I do not understand it."

Even worse, thought Darius.

He couldn't dare tell Pheus, not facing his cold glare. With his arms crossed, the priest lifted his chin and turned as if the very sight of Jerico angered him. Darius tried to think of an excuse, but he knew none, and he stared at the ground in shame.

"I thought so," said Pheus. He sighed, and his anger retreated into sadness. "I pity you, Darius. You have great potential, though more than ever I fear you will waste it. But perhaps I see only the weakness I fear; it is a curse my colleagues have often berated me for. This is a joyous occasion, and I come spreading the word to all the faithful."

"And what is that?" Darius asked, glad to have the conversation changed.

"The Citadel has fallen. The paladins of Ashhur are scattered, homeless, with many casting aside their faith. Our time of victory has come. The Stronghold has declared war upon the survivors, every last one."

Darius's jaw dropped. He thought of Jerico's attempt to leave the day before, and suddenly he understood.

"How?" he asked, still struggling to believe it.

"The Voice of the Lion led the assault, and through his disciple Xelrak, brought the building crashing to the ground. I have been traveling north to inform all I can of our new orders. Ashhur's paladins are weak now, helpless. We must descend upon them before they regroup."

"Wait...you want to kill Jerico?"

"Kill him? No. We want him *executed* for his blasphemy and service to the false god. Do you not understand? After all these years, we have a chance for complete victory." He pointed toward Jerico, and it seemed as if his eyes sparkled.

"For all I know, he is the very last. Let us take him now, before he realizes the danger he is in."

"No," Darius said, stepping away. "Do you not see the chaos about us? Wolf-men gather in great numbers beyond the Gihon, and any day they will swim across. They'll slaughter every one of these villagers. Jerico stands at my side. For now, if any of us are to live, we need him."

Pheus leaned back against the tree. For a long minute he did not speak, only stare, as if gazing into the depths of Darius's soul. Whatever he saw there, he certainly did not like.

"This is your failure," Pheus said at last. "And it is yours to correct. This…Jerico…will die by your hand. That is an order, and you will obey, paladin."

He left the tree and wrapped an arm around Darius's shoulder. "I must continue my travels. By the time I return, I expect the matter handled. If it is not, the Stronghold will hear of your failure. I assure you, they will be far less understanding than I."

"Will you not stay and help us?"

"This village is your responsibility, not mine. These men are of the earth, and there will always be a thousand others like them. Our war with Ashhur has waged for hundreds of years. Do you think I would risk losing that over a handful of farmers? What you do, do quickly, Darius. I have spoken. Obey your god."

Pheus left along the northern road, not a single man or woman saying a word in greeting as he passed by. Darius watched him go, and he stared long after he was gone.

"You all right?" Jerico asked him, having returned to the square after doing who knew what to help another family.

Darius looked at the man, tired, proud, his red hair soaked with sweat and covered with dirt. He tried to see him as an enemy, a blasphemer of a false god. Instead, he saw Jerico. *I fear your reaction should you face a true challenge of Ashhur,* Pheus had said two years ago, and it seemed prophetic. Was Jerico such a challenge? Had he prepared for physical strength, skill in combat, and left his heart unprepared for the lies, the facades, the tempting half-truths of Ashhur? How could he follow Karak, yet claim a paladin of Ashhur as his friend?

"I'm fine," he said.

"If you say. The Douglas family needs help fixing their wagon for the journey. Can you help them out?"

Darius nodded, still feeling as if he walked in a troubled dream.

"Jerico," he said, stopping the other paladin from leaving. "I…forgive me. The Citadel. Have you heard?"

Jerico's face paled, he swallowed, but he nodded.

"I'm sorry," Darius said, unsure if it were truth or lie.

"Go help Jim and his wagon. And Darius…thank you."

A cruel, chaotic world, thought Darius. What greater proof could he need?

Jacob Wheatley bent over beside the wheelbarrow in his garden, swearing at each passing moment. He yanked and tore at the zucchini and winter squash. The tiny hairs on their sides poked his hands, and several cuts bled along his thumbs and palm. Under the best circumstances he wasn't a patient man, and today he had even less time to be careful. The wolf-men were coming, and the whole town was turning yellow and running.

"Can't believe Jeremy's such a bloody coward," he muttered. "Would probably tuck his dick between his legs and run from a fucking rabbit if it bared its teeth."

"They ain't no rabbits," said Perry, son of his neighbor, Jim Douglas. Jacob usually paid the boy a few coppers to help with his harvest, along with a bottle of shine his father knew nothing about. The two had already filled one wheelbarrow, dumped it back at his house, and come back for a second load.

"Shit, I know that, son. I was there with everyone else when we stepped into the wedge. We were in their land, at night, and we still gave as good as we got. Thank the gods those paladins were there, though. I mean, you should have seen what Gary looked like before the redheaded one could heal...hey, you listening?"

Perry stood straight, a yellow squash still in his hand. His eyes scanned the distance with an intensity that riled up the snakes in Jacob's stomach.

"I said you listening?" he asked, louder.

"I saw something. There. I'm sure of it."

"What could you be seeing?" Jacob asked, looking. He saw the edge of his garden, then the long stretch of hills, followed by the slender forest. "There ain't nothing out there."

"I was *sure*," Perry insisted.

"And I was sure Tessie would marry me if I bought her a ring. Sometimes we're so sure of something we don't realize how stupid we are. At least that tease ended up with Noel. Don't tell your pap, but I hear his dick's the size of a..."

"*There!*"

Jacob stood a second time, and he followed Perry's outstretched arm. This time he did see a vague shape, but only for a few heartbeats before it sank back into the grass.

"What the fuck was that?" asked Jacob.

"Dog maybe? Looked gray..."

"Dog?" Jacob felt his blood chill. "How big a dog, you think?"

Perry realized what he thought, and he paled.

"It's daylight," he said, as if that should mean anything. Jacob glanced behind him. In the far distance was his house, and several hundred yards beyond, the Douglas home. He could make out vague shapes in front of their porch, no doubt Jim trying to fix that damn wagon of his. He'd made excuses all summer, and now he was learning a hard lesson about putting off until tomorrow what you should have done two weeks ago.

"It's a long run," Jacob said, his voice low. "But we might have to do it anyway. You still watching?"

"Yeah."

Jacob knelt and pulled a few more squashes, struggling to not look alert.

"You just act like you're catching your breath. Wait for it to move again. Don't stare at it, you idiot. Look away. Use the corner of your eye, as if you're trying to peep down a girl's blouse without her knowin' it."

Perry's neck went red, but he nodded and tried to obey. Jacob counted the seconds, wishing the damn thing, whatever it was, would hurry up and make its move.

"It crawled again," Perry said suddenly. "Shit, it's big."

"It stopped?"

"Yeah."

"Then run like the wind, boy."

Jacob stood, grabbed the handles of his wheelbarrow, and ran. Perry had the shorter legs, but he was a wiry boy and unencumbered. Gradually he pulled ahead. Jacob felt the wheelbarrow jostle in his hands. His vegetables would be bruised beyond recognition, but by the gods he wasn't leaving them behind. It was a matter of pride. He glanced back once, hoping to be revealed an idiot, to see nothing behind him but his empty garden.

A gray wolf-man loped after them, its back bent, its tongue hanging out the side of its mouth.

"Fuck!" he shouted, turning back around. "Run, goddamn it, Perry, *run!*"

But the boy was getting tired, his short legs working double-time to keep pace, and they were only halfway down the path toward his home. For a moment he considered tossing Perry into the wheelbarrow, but he knew that'd only get them both killed. No time…no time! He slowed, then stopped completely.

"Jacob?" Perry asked, whirling about. His eyes widened, and Jacob knew he saw their pursuer.

"You not hear me? I said run, you twat, now run!"

Perry obeyed. Swallowing his fear, Jacob turned to face the wolf-man. It was closing the distance between them with horrifying speed. Giddy laughter bubbled up from his belly, and he couldn't hold it in. Here he was, facing off against one of the most terrifying creatures of all Dezrel, and his only weapon was a wheelbarrow. He was fucked. Totally, completely fucked.

The wolf-man seemed to share the sentiment, for it howled with joy just before leaping at him. Jacob dropped to his knees, ramming his arms against the wheelbarrow's handles. It pivoted into the air on the back braces. In mid-jump, the wolf couldn't change its angle in time. It rammed its chest against the front, which crumpled inward with a metallic groan. Its momentum killed, it fell back onto its hind legs, the wheelbarrow tipping over onto its side. Jacob dove for it, curling his legs to his chest as he lay atop a pile of vegetables.

Snarling, the wolf-man yanked the remnants of his wheelbarrow off him, removing whatever defense he had.

Still laughing, Jacob swung the biggest squash he could find. It smacked against the wolf-man's nose. Blood sprayed across him, and he wondered what had made the crunching noise, the thing's nose or the shattered squash in his hand. As the wolf staggered back, swinging its head back and forth in a daze, Jacob took to his feet and ran. He knew it would only be a few extra seconds, but he had to try. In the brief moment, he realized he couldn't see Perry, and he figured that enough of a victory. The boy would survive, at least longer than Jacob was going to. If the entire pack had come early, then they were all destined for a stay in a cramped belly.

When the wolf-man hit him, it felt like a sledgehammer had slammed his back. He flew through the air, his arms and legs waving wildly. The ground rushed toward him, and it seemed like his legs couldn't find purchase to keep running. He braced his fall best he could, then rolled along the rough ground. As rocks tore into his skin, he screamed. It felt like his back was on fire. When he came to a stop, the wolf-man towered over him, blood trickling down its nose and onto its yellow teeth.

"I'll eat you slowly," it said, its hot breath washing over him. "I'll eat you alive."

"Shut up and do it," Jacob said. The world seemed to swirl before him, and he felt like the patch of ground he lay upon was unstable. Light-headed, he watched with strange disinterest as the wolf-men brought its gaping maw to his chest and bit. Warm blood spilled to his abdomen, and he heard someone screaming. It was him, he realized. That was embarrassing. He'd always thought himself tougher than that.

The wolf-man pinned his arms, because evidently he'd been struggling. It grinned at him, its whole mouth dripping red. It swallowed something. A piece of his flesh. A soft growl came from its throat, and it sounded hungry. Claws dug into his wrists. More screaming.

And then he realized he must have begun hallucinating, for the wolf-man's head suddenly vanished, replaced by a stump that spurted blood into his eyes. He cried out and shut them, hating the sting. The pressure on his wrists vanished. People were talking, he realized, and he made an effort to listen.

"...too badly, Jacob. Sorry I don't have time to stitch your chest. You'll have to make do with a tight cloth."

"No bother," Jacob said, the dreamlike feel growing. "Is it still going to eat me?"

Dark laughter met his ears.

"It is dead, though I fear it's not the only one we have to worry about. Take my arm and stand."

Jacob felt something grab him, lifting him by his armpits. Once righted, he felt his weight rest on his feet, and he struggled to maintain balance. His strange savior held him steady, and ignoring the biting pain in his eyes, he opened them to look. The dark paladin, Darius, leaned his weight against him, and together they walked back to his home.

"Perry got to me just in time," Darius said, picking up their pace. "Your back's a mess, and your chest is bleeding like a stuck pig, but I'm not giving you any choice. You're going to walk, you're going to live, and you're going to remember to tithe every week whether you feel like it or not."

"Will two of three do?" Jacob asked.

His savior laughed. "For now."

Perry was waiting for him at the house, his face wet with tears and covered with dirt. His father was with him, along with his damned wagon. They'd already loaded his vegetables, he realized. That was kind of them.

"You're all right," Perry said, the relief palpable.

"Don't feel it."

They laid him in the wagon, pushing aside rickety crates of food and clothing to make room. Darius gave the order and the wagon began moving. Perry hopped in with him, holding a long rag.

"He said to tie this around you," the kid said.

"Then do it."

Jacob grunted as the cloth slid around his chest. It didn't take long for it to turn a dark crimson, but the pressure felt good. Leaning back, Jacob closed his eyes, drowsiness overcoming him.

"There was another," Perry said, talking out of nervousness. "Back at my pa's house. If Darius hadn't been there, if he…"

"Perry?"

"Yeah?"

"Shut up, will ya? We're going to be fine."

He opened an eye to see the kid smiling at him. It was a thin mask, a tiny strength covering a massive wall of fear, but at least it was something.

"Should have known a single wolf-man wouldn't kill you," Perry said. "You're too stubborn for that."

"Too stupid's more like it. So is this it? This the big attack?"

Perry's smile wavered, but he managed to keep it there.

"Nah. Darius said it ain't."

"Then what is it? You got any ideas, boy?"

Apparently he didn't, for he only shrugged. Jacob leaned back, moaning occasionally as the wagon bounced along.

"Jacob?"

"Yeah?"

Perry looked away.

"Thanks for saving me."
Jacob slapped the boy's leg, then lay back down.
"Was nothing," he said. "Nothing…"
He slept despite the pain and movement of the wagon.

9

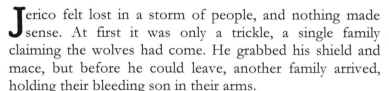

Jerico felt lost in a storm of people, and nothing made sense. At first it was only a trickle, a single family claiming the wolves had come. He grabbed his shield and mace, but before he could leave, another family arrived, holding their bleeding son in their arms.

"Two of 'em!" the father cried. "They got Terry. They got my son!"

Fearing the full attack to come, he sought out Darius. Not finding him, he instead located Daniel and his men, who had also prepared themselves for battle.

"Death may be coming for us," Daniel said, "but we'll meet it armed and ready. Gods willing, we'll take plenty of them with us!"

They marched to the center of town, and that was when Jerico found Darius. He waited there, looking strangely calm amid the din. People were shouting, asking questions. He ignored them all.

"Jerico," he said, seeing him. "Two attacked the outer farms, Douglas and Wheatley. I saw more, but they kept back, circling."

"Why didn't you chase them down, then?" Daniel asked, pushing people aside to join them.

"Because I am no fool," Darius said, glaring at the older man. "They're circling, don't you get it? We're completely cut off from the world. Every road, every farm, even the river...the wolf-men watch them all."

The realization hit Jerico like a blow from his own mace.

"We're trapped," he whispered. "What do we tell the people? What do we do?"

"My baby!" a mother wailed behind them. Jerico couldn't think of her name. She was a lost face in a sea of frightened villagers. Several more wandered about, bleeding, and Jerico saw the wounded man in a cart sitting beside him in the square.

"We need to get the wounded somewhere," he said. "I can heal them, though it'll take much of my strength."

"The attack isn't coming today," Daniel said. "You have time."

"How do you know?"

"Because if it was coming today, they'd bloody well do it. They've given us warning now, which does them no good. That means they plan on keeping us here, nice and quiet, while they starve us, weaken and frighten us."

Jerico glanced to Darius, who nodded in agreement.

"Move the wounded to the inn," said the dark paladin. "I'll check the roads north. Daniel, send men to check the south. Have the rest try to keep order here. We need to take stock of what we have, in both food and weaponry. If they're to trap us, then we need to lay a trap right back. We are the cornered animal, gentlemen, so let's act like it."

Jerico stepped back, pushing his way toward Dolores's inn.

"Bring your wounded!" he shouted to them. "All hurt, all bleeding, come to me at Dolores's!"

Inside he found Dolores sitting on a stool, her hands crossed on her lap. She was crying.

"We're all to die, aren't we?" she asked.

"Someday," Jerico said, clearing space on the floor. "But not today."

"I'm not scared of dying," she said as the first of many followed, carrying wounded or bearing wounds themselves. "But to die to them...to be alive when they...they..."

"Dolores!" Jerico looked at her, refusing to let his gaze falter. She stared at him, tears running down her face, and her old lips quivered. "Not now. Not ever. Help me, please. Blankets, bandages, and towels for the blood. Your passing will be in your sleep, even older, and even crankier. You think a damn wolf can chew through your leathery hide?"

She smiled at him, and whatever daze she'd been in crumbled.

"Lay 'em the other way," she said as Jerico put the first down. "More room. Ugh, so much blood. You got a needle for stitches?"

"Something like that," Jerico said, closing his eyes and putting his hands on a man's chest, lined with eight vicious cuts. Where his fingers touched skin they glowed with white light, and after a quiet moment, the light plunged within, smoothing over the flesh and knitting torn muscle.

More and more came in, crowding the small inn. Dolores guided them to corners, and she wrapped blankets across those Jerico healed. The sobs of both healthy and sick echoed upon the walls.

"Jerico!" a boy cried out. He glanced that way, saw Perry kneeling over Jacob Wheatley.

"Close your eyes and be strong," Jerico whispered to a woman who had lost her arm. He'd closed the wound and wrapped it with a bandage, the best he could do. Walking to Perry, he stopped a moment, a dizzy spell coming over him.

"He stayed back 'cause I couldn't keep up," Perry said, glancing down at Jacob. "You'll help him, won't you? I don't want him...him...he can't die. It'll be all my fault. My fault!"

Jerico knelt to examine the wounds. His back was bleeding, but it appeared to be from shallow slashes that would only prove fatal if they became infected. The bite on his chest, however...

"Be with him," Jerico prayed, his hands on the rupture. The blood felt hot on his fingers. The light bathed over them both. Slowly, the change unseen through the light, the skin closed into a long, angry scar. When finished, Jerico leaned against the wall and gasped. So many. He had never been the greatest at healing, and facing so many wounded, so many clawed and mangled people...

"Come on," Dolores said, offering her hand. He took it and stood.

"I have needle and thread," she continued. "Save those beyond all but Ashhur. The rest, well, they can do with a bit of stitching for now."

"Thank you," he muttered.

They triaged the worst, Jerico praying at their sides to close gaping wounds while Dolores moved about, sewing shut minor cuts and applying tourniquets when it was clear the limb was lost. By the time he was done, there were forty men, women, and children lying on the floor in blankets, with the lesser wounded staying in various rooms, including Darius's. Seven died, and quietly Jerico took them behind the inn for eventual burial.

They cleared out every piece of furniture but for two chairs, and Jerico sat in one beside Dolores, looking over the many. They were crying, sleeping, or staring into the distance. Dolores had had to force all family members out. In some ways, that had been the worst. No matter how often Jerico told them there was no room, that they had to leave, they still sobbed, still clutched at their loved ones as if they might never see them again. Breaking that up felt wrong, but he knew it must be done.

"Jerico?"

The paladin glanced up to see Darius standing at the door. He gestured outside, and Jerico nodded.

"Will you watch them?" he asked Dolores.

"Go on," she said. "You have much to do, but don't push yourself. Hate to find you on my floor with the others."

Jerico stepped carefully among the bodies, then followed Darius outside. Daniel had returned, though his men were still hurrying about the town. Things had calmed down, but only a little. It seemed like everyone had a task set before them, and that kept down the bulk of the panic.

"So what's the story?" he asked.

"Patrols to both directions," Darius said, and Daniel nodded in agreement.

Jerico sighed, wishing he was a cussing man. He knew plenty that felt appropriate for the situation

"Where's Jeremy Hangfield?"

"Taking stock of our supplies," Daniel said. "We got lucky. With everyone preparing to move out, most had gathered up their belongings and brought them into town already. Because of this, we got plenty of food to live on, at least for a week or two. If they plan on starving us out, it'll take time, time I doubt they have. Sir Godley will notice something is up, if not one of the other towers."

Jerico caught sight of a man in black robes approaching, and he raised an eyebrow.

"That your friend?" he asked Darius. The paladin turned, and seeing the man, bowed on one knee in respect.

"Pheus, you've returned to us," he said.

"I have," said the priest, glaring at Jerico. "Two wolf-men accosted me on the northern road."

"How did you escape?" Jerico asked.

Pheus gave him a look of such contempt it chilled his blood.

"I killed them, of course."

"We'll need all the help we can get," Darius said. "And the question is, do we hunker down, or try to punch through their circle?"

"They'll harry us for miles," Jerico said, shaking his head. "No matter which direction we go, it sounds like they'll be watching. Our best chance now is to protect ourselves and hope someone notices our isolation; the traders they attacked last night, perhaps."

"What about sending off a boat for aid?" Daniel asked. "Down south to the nearest tower, or better yet, to the Citadel?"

Jerico winced, and he saw both priest and paladin of Karak look his way. Darius's eyes revealed nothing, though Pheus was clearly amused.

"The Citadel is no more," Jerico said. "We will get no aid from them."

He turned to leave. A hand grabbed his shoulder, and he spun, his hand reaching for his weapon. Darius pulled away, and he looked at the mace with a mixture of betrayal and anger.

"I wanted to thank you for what you did in there," he said, gesturing to the inn. His voice lacked what conviction it might have had, though. Jerico released the handle of his mace and nodded.

"We'll gather everyone into a few places to sleep," Daniel said, glancing between them. He clearly felt the tension in the air, and he pushed on to change the subject. "Will make it easier keeping watch. Need to get our food into safe places too, so they can't destroy it. Oh, and last of all, we need to stay off each other's throats. Times before a battle can make even the kindest men turn to ogres. Let's all remember that, eh?"

"I have wounded to attend," Jerico said. "Excuse me."

He returned to the inn, feeling both furious and embarrassed by that fury. Darius had meant no insult, yet he felt hot under the collar anyway. It was just the way that priest stared at him, with a mocking glint. No doubt he'd cheered when the Citadel fell. No doubt he expected Darius to feel the same way. Did he?

"Any news worth sharing?" Dolores asked him, keeping her voice low so as not to wake the sleeping.

"No," he said. "What hope we have is little."

She frowned.

"Out in the back," she said. "Will you take care of 'em?"

He sighed. His temples throbbed, his forehead ached with every heartbeat, but still he nodded.

"Might be the only chance we have to bury our dead," he murmured.

"Don't you talk like that," Dolores said. "Not where they can hear. Thought you smarter than that."

Jerico accepted the berating in silence, then left the inn once more.

At Jeremy's mansion he found a shovel, and he brought it with him to the inn. There was plenty of open space behind it. Normally the people of Durham buried their dead at the corners of the fields, returning them to the ground that allowed them to prosper. There would be no such act, not with the wolves closing in. The ground was soft enough, and he dug the first of many graves. After he was done with the second, and the sun started its descent, coloring the sky pink, Darius arrived. The dark paladin watched for a moment, left, and then returned with another shovel. Jerico put the bodies in, and Darius covered them up. This they did until the seventh, and both stabbed their shovels into the ground and leaned their weight against them.

"I'm sorry about the Citadel," Darius said.

"Are you?"

Darius sighed, and he looked away. When he looked back, he knew for certain his answer.

"Yes. I am."

Jerico gestured to the graves.

"Hundreds of my brethren died. I saw them in a vision, granted to me by Ashhur. No one will dig them graves. No one will gather before them to mourn. The dead tore apart their bodies and cast them to the dirt. Who deserves such a fate? Who would hate us so?"

The Voice of the Lion, Pheus had said. Darius knew that name, though he had never met him. The fabled prophet of Karak, his priest since before the Gods' War. Eyes of blood and fire, and never the same face. He was a relic of a more fanatical time. At the Stronghold, Darius had been taught to honor him should they ever meet, for none were supposed to be closer to their deity. And now he had brought low the Citadel. Would Jerico understand? Could he? Were they truly at war, and Jerico an enemy he had befriended?

"I fear whatever answer I might give will offer no satisfaction," he said.

"You're probably right. Every part of me wants to leave, to go to the rubble and see it for myself. I don't want to believe it. I might never, really, until I see the wreckage. How could...how could Ashhur abandon us so?"

The crisis of faith seemed too personal, too close to home for Darius. He turned away and gestured to the setting sun.

"We should go inside and rest. Unless the wolf-men are exceptionally clever, they'll attack at night, which will be when you and I must stand guard. It'll be a long night, and following a long day, but we'll endure. Won't you, Jerico?"

Jerico stood and clapped Darius on the shoulder.

"Forgive my behavior, Darius. I'm tired, scared, and sad. That priest of yours, when I see him looking at me...I feel more alone than ever. And hated, too. I never should have disrespected you so."

"All's forgiven," Darius said. "I'll be with the wounded at the inn. Daniel's men are watching Jeremy's estate. That leaves the tavern for you."

"Thank you," Jerico said.

"For?"

In answer, he gestured to the mounds of dirt, the only marker for the seven dead.

"Think nothing of it," said Darius. "They won't be the last. Together, life and death, the fate of the village rests in our hands, both yours and mine. Peaceful nights, Jerico."

"To you as well."

They split for their respective assignments.

She'd always liked the privacy of her room, and that's what Jessie Hangfield missed most of all. Keeping her bed to herself had required little argument, but three other women slept on the floor. They shuffled, cried, and snored. Every noise bothered Jessie to no end. There were summer nights where even the song of the cicadas could keep her staring at her ceiling for hours. Hearing such inconsistent noises breaking the quiet only reminded her she was not alone, and not yet asleep despite how tired she felt.

Jessie shifted to her side and stared out the window of her room. The glass was recently cleaned, product of a strange delusion that she should tidy up the place before the swarm of guests invaded her father's home. It was only when the women arrived that she realized how stupid she'd been. A pink talking rabbit could have greeted them at the door, and they still would have thought nothing of it. Their eyes were wide, but seeing nothing. She knew them all, and she felt too scared to ask them of their families.

"Blessed of the light, watch over me," she heard Lyla pray. Lyla was beside her bed, wrapped in a thin blanket she'd brought from her home. It was the fifth time she'd begun the ritual prayer to Ashhur. No matter that others were trying to sleep. It seemed that ritual cadence was the only thing keeping her sane. She was not that much older than Jessie, with a handsome husband and a newborn babe. No amount of courage could have convinced her to ask where they were, nor ask her to be quiet.

So she shouted it mentally. Shut up, shut up, shut up! It was unfair, absurdly unfair, but this was her room. She wanted to bury her face in her pillow and scream until her lungs gave out, to cry until her pillow could take no more tears. Every noise she heard made her heart stop. Every weird creak was the step of a wolf. Jessie could imagine one leering over her, its mouth drooling, its yellow eyes glowing in the darkness. Tears ran down her face, and she wiped them with a blanket. Lyla began her prayer for the sixth time. Jessie whispered the words along this time, begging Ashhur to let her sleep, to let her forget the day's horror for only a few blissful hours.

Granny Jane slept by the door. As if on clockwork, she rolled from her left side to her right every ten minutes. She snored loud, long, and with enough depth that Jessie thought it could pass for the growl of a bear. Her husband had died several years back, and as Jessie wiped tears from her face she wondered how in the world Granny's husband had endured those many nights. Maybe he'd wedged cotton into his ears, or better yet, candle wax. That's what she should have done. Despite her exhaustion, she pondered leaving her bedroom and searching the kitchen for some wax to use. But no matter how much she wanted to, she never worked up the nerve. The reason was stupid, she knew, but in her exhausted mind it didn't seem to matter. She didn't want to offend her guests, or make them feel they were unwanted. Because in truth she wasn't a selfish girl, and she knew they'd all suffered far worse than her that day.

"Blessed of the light, watch over me. May I walk your road and never stray..."

A shape blocked the window, a small part of it glinting yellow. Jessie screamed. The window smashed open. As the shards fell, the wolf-man crashed atop of Lyla, its claws flinging blood in wild arcs across the room. Jessie screamed again, and blood splashed across her face, stinging her eyes. Lyla, poor Lyla...this couldn't be happening. Her mind refused to believe it.

The third guest, a midwife named Wilma, bolted to a sit, screaming as well. She turned to crawl, her portly body nearly smothering Granny Jane on her way to the door. The wolf-man would have none of it. It leapt atop her next, its teeth sinking into the fat of her back. Jessie felt her bladder let go. The creature was so huge, and it flung Wilma's head side to side, snapping her neck. The sound it made, like a heavy branch breaking on someone's knee, spurred her to action. She rolled off the bed, away from the door. She didn't want the thing to see her. That was all she could think of, that infantile desire to hide.

The thing snarled, and suddenly she found breathing difficult. The opposite side of the bed was not enough. She crawled underneath, quietly sobbing the whole while. As if from a hundred miles away, she heard shouts from further within her father's house. Granny knelt against the door, her mouth open and her eyes wide. Her left arm reached for the knob, flailing at it wildly as if she'd forgotten how the contraption worked.

"Get out of here!" Granny shouted. At first Jessie thought she shouted at the beast, but then realized it was to her she cried. "The window, out now!"

Granny held the doorknob tight, and when the wolf-men tore into her, she never let go. Unable to stop crying, Jessie looked away and crawled for the other side. The window...the glass was shattered from the creature's arrival. If she could sneak out and hide, she might survive. Stumbling onto her feet, she ran for it, unafraid of the jagged edges of glass that remained. Shards littered the floor as well, and they cut her bare feet. Something tripped her, and she cried out. Lyla's body. They stared face to face, noses almost touching. Panic gave her speed she didn't know she possessed. Her hands clawed at the window, and up she went, thinking only of escape. Something tugged her dressed, she fought, and then she was flying.

"No!" she shrieked at the top of her lungs, landing atop her piss-soaked bed. The wolf-man towered over her, blood on its claws and pieces of flesh hanging from its teeth.

"Four for Yellowscar," it snarled, reaching for her throat.

The door burst inward, and in the distraction, Jessie dove once more to the ground. She rolled under the bed, her arms tucked against her chest. She closed her eyes and wished she could blot out the sounds. The wolf-man snarled, but several men were crying out. Steel hit claw, and daring to open her eyes, she saw the soldiers from Blood Tower had come. The wolf twisted and struck, but every time she heard it scrape against something, a shield perhaps, or maybe their armor. Another set of legs came through the open door. She wanted to run for it, but she feared getting in their way. Not knowing what else to do, she prayed the same cadence, her heart aching for poor Lyla.

"Blessed of the light, watch over me."

A man cried out. Blood splashed to the floor.

"May I walk your road and never stray."

The soldier hit the ground, his head facing hers. Air leaked from his torn throat.

"May I feel your arms around me when I fall."

The life in his eyes faded, his arms twitching their last. The wolf-man growled deep.

May I sing your praises when I stand.

More cries. The legs of the soldiers surrounded the wolf, and she heard it yelp in pain.

Blessed of the light, may I love you, as you have always loved me.

A hand reached for her under the bed, and she took it. Crawling out, she looked up to see her father.

"Daddy," she cried, flinging her arms around him and sobbing into his chest.

"There, there," Jeremy said, stroking her head as beside her the soldiers dragged the bleeding, bound body of the wolf-man from the room.

She never wanted him to let her go.

Night of Wolves

10

"**A**re you sure there are no more?" Jerico asked as he followed the soldier through the town toward the Hangfield home.

"Fairly sure," said the soldier. "It crashed through the window of Jeremy's girl. Killed three before we got there, and another before we could get it down. We've got it tied up in Jeremy's cellar. So far it hasn't said a word."

"Jessie...is she all right?"

Jerico felt his heart pause for a moment as the soldier thought, but then he nodded.

"Yeah. I remember seeing her crying in her father's arms. She looked fine. Well, fine as circumstances allowed, if you get my meaning."

The paladin breathed a sigh of relief.

"She's a good soul," he said. "I'd hate for something to happen to her."

"Four others died instead of her," the soldier said, halting before Jeremy's house. "One of 'em was my friend. You saying they *ain't* good souls?"

Jerico flushed, and embarrassed, he shook his head.

"Forgive me. I was wrong. What is your name, soldier?"

The man gave him a look, then nodded.

"All right. I see we understand each other. My name's Gregory. Pleased to meet you."

"Likewise," Jerico muttered as they entered through the front door.

Jeremy was waiting for them, standing in his robes by the door. With him in the small room was his daughter, sitting in a chair near the corner. Her eyes were closed, and she rocked the chair back and forth with gentle pushes of her foot.

"Glad you're here," Jeremy said. "Darius and his, uh, friend are already down there, and I don't like the sounds I'm hearing."

"Sounds?" Jerico asked.

The man only shrugged and pointed them toward the musty door leading to the cellar. Gregory led the way. Halfway down he heard a strange shriek, and he realized it was the wolf-man crying out in agony. The sound made his skin crawl, and he pitied the others throughout the large house still trying to sleep. Jerico braced himself for the scene he knew he'd encounter, but was still unprepared for the brutality of it.

The wolf-man lay flat on the floor, this feat accomplished by the breaking of its knees so they might bend the necessary way, instead of backwards like a wolf's. Ropes lashed across its body, nailed into the hard earth of the cellar. Patches of its skin were missing, as if burned, though he saw only a single torch hung upon the wall. Blood seeped across its body from a multitude of wounds. Pheus stood over it, shadows dancing across his fingers. Darius stood at his side. Watching with three of his men was Daniel, his arms crossed and his expression revealing nothing. The shadows dipped into the wolf-man's flesh. It pulled against the ropes holding it, every muscle twitching chaotically.

"What is this?" Jerico asked, feeling stupid even as he said it.

"No business of yours," said Pheus. "We have information to learn from this mongrel. Daniel's soldiers were wise in keeping it alive, and should be commended for such quick thinking."

Daniel scowled, clearly unimpressed with the compliment.

"You're letting him torture it?" Jerico asked him.

"Three helpless women dead," Daniel said, looking away. "Plus one of my men. Go take a look at Jessie's room if you want to see why I let them be. The walls are painted red."

Jerico glared at Darius, but the man returned his gaze unflinching.

"All our lives may depend on this," said the dark paladin.

"Enough," said Pheus. He knelt down and placed his hands on either side of the wolf-man's head. "It is time you talk. Tell me your name, or you will feel pain a thousand times greater than you have felt before."

"Yellowscar," the creature whimpered. Its eyes were unfocused, with the whites of one turned pink and covered with veins.

"Very well, Yellowscar. Why did you kill those women? Were you under order?"

The creature made a strange sound. Jerico couldn't decide if it were a laugh or a growl.

"I killed for honor."

"Honor?" Daniel spat. "You killed helpless women for *honor?*"

Yellowscar tilted its head so it could stare at him with its good eye. The pink one didn't move with the other.

"You are weak. Human. You know nothing of honor."

"Is that so?" Pheus said. He struck Yellowscar's snout with his palm. Dark energy flowed into it, and the wolf-man yelped at the top of its lungs, a cry that stretched on for what felt like an eternity.

"Enough!" Jerico cried, not to the wolf, but to Pheus.

"You would challenge me?" the priest asked. Instead of angry, he appeared almost delighted by the prospect.

"I won't watch you torture this poor creature."

"Then leave," said Darius. "You know this must be done."

Jerico felt all eyes upon him, and he struggled to decide what was right. This creature might know when the attack would come. But making it suffer and howl while above children slept...it wasn't right. He stepped toward Yellowscar, his motions careful. Black stars sparkled on the edge of Pheus's fingertips, and he seemed eager for the slightest excuse to let them fly. Kneeling beside the wolf-man, Jerico put his hands on the worst of the creature's wounds and prayed for the pain to stop.

"Rest," he said to it, his voice low, reassuring. "Now listen. You have murdered our own, and no matter how this night ends, you will die for those crimes. We know who leads your pack. Redclaw, isn't it? I've looked upon him. I've seen his strength, and when he comes to kill us, I will face him. I will bring him down. But before I do, I will tell him Yellowscar died a warrior. When will your pack attack Durham? Tell me, and I will end your suffering. The blood will be on my hands, not theirs. No torture. No pain. This is your one chance, Yellowscar. This is all I can promise, for beyond this is uncertain."

Yellowscar looked at him, glancing only once at Pheus and his eager, painful touch.

"You are of honor," it told him. "You I will trust. I will speak, but do not kill me here. Do not kill Yellowscar in ropes. Fight me beneath the moon so I may die a warrior."

Jerico glanced at Daniel, who scratched his chin.

"Fair enough," he said. "His legs are broke. He ain't running off like that."

"You cause us unnecessary delay," Pheus argued.

"A delay, perhaps," said Jerico.

The wolf-man's hands were already bound together at the wrist, but its mouth still posed a threat. Darius wrapped a rope around it thrice, then knotted it behind Yellowscar's head. He gestured to Daniel, letting him know he was all his.

"No," Jerico said, stepping forward. "I will carry him."

The wolf-man was heavy, and though he braced his weight on his shoulder, it was still agony standing. Despite his protest, Gregory stepped forward and took half the burden. Each holding an arm, Yellowscar's legs trailing uselessly against the floor, they carried him up the stairs and into the night. The rest followed.

"He cannot stand," Gregory said when they let go.

"Untie him anyway. We shall see."

Watching him closely, Jerico cut the bonds around the wrists. Ashhur cried no soft warning in his head, so he did not flinch at their freedom. He removed the muzzle next. Done, he stepped back and pulled his shield off his back, the glow lighting up the darkness. He would not need it, but neither would he shame Yellowscar by handicapping himself.

"Stand, Yellowscar," he said, drawing his mace.

The rest watched, keeping silent. The creature groaned, then rolled onto its stomach. Its heavy arms pushed itself to a sit. Its tongue hung from the side of its mouth, and every muscle in its body quivered.

"I said stand."

One leg propped underneath, followed by the other. The joints snapped, the bones shifting back the way they belonged. Yellowscar howled, but did not fall. Inch by inch he rose, great shuddering breaths thundering out of his mouth.

"Redclaw attacks come the full moon," he said, each word a labor. "And they will feast, and sing, and never return to the Wedge."

Jerico felt the words in his head, and with an innate power of Ashhur, he tested to see if they were true. They were. He glanced at Daniel, nodded, and then took a step forward.

"Strike me, creature of the Wedge."

Yellowscar cried out, for one brief moment sounding like the furious creature he was. His claws lashed out, slapping across Jerico's shield. The paladin stepped in, swung his mace, and then closed his eyes as the metal struck bone. Yellowscar dropped to the ground, blood oozing from his jaw and empty eye socket.

"About damn time," Darius muttered.

Jerico glared.

"We have two days," Daniel said. He breathed in deep and then sighed, as if a great weight had lifted from his shoulders. "Now we know. Now we prepare. This is your mess, Jerico. I trust you to bury it."

Daniel took his men and left. Pheus frowned at the corpse.

"Yellowscar was a heartless, brutal killer," the priest said. "You give honor to what has none. You bow to the wishes of a beaten foe. Your kind is weak, Jerico, and full of fools. A shame the world may never learn this, for when the last paladin of Ashhur fades away, how will they ever see for themselves?"

He left, leaving only Darius and Jerico standing beside the body.

"I expected better from you," Jerico said.

"You know nothing of me. Your own damn fault."

He turned to leave, but Jerico stopped him.

"What did he mean, when we fade away?"

Darius opened his mouth, then closed it. He looked away, clearly troubled.

"Darius?"

"What?"

Jerico put a hand on his shoulder. "Will you help me bury him?"

The dark paladin sighed.

"Yes. I will, though I doubt even Karak knows why."

Redclaw had discussed battle with his elders while growing up as a pup, and in turn, spoken with those now sworn to his name. Nearly all talked of eagerness, the swelling of fury and triumph as they raced for a kill. It was almost a madness, a desire unparalleled to taste the blood of their foe. In this, Redclaw had learned from an early age how different he was, how weak. When he howled to the night sky, it was because he tried to hide his fear. When he raced ahead of his pack to be the first into bloodshed, it was because he knew the moment he felt his claws sink into the flesh of his opponent, his instincts would take over. It was only then, when he lost himself amid the chaos, that he felt his nerves calm.

That same nervous fear swelled in him as he waited for Bloodfang and Murdertongue to arrive at the Gathering.

Outwardly he exuded nothing but confidence. He wondered if his pack could smell the scent of shame upon him, betraying him. So far none had dared ask, and he himself had never detected it. Every time he thought of being the moon made flesh, of being the Wolf King, he remembered his fear, and he wondered how worthy he was of the title. A glance at his pups, watching him from the first row with Bonebite lurking protectively over them, gave him the strength to continue. They would not remain in the Wedge, trapped with other animals in a crowded cage. They would not be raised on tough meat and foul water.

Moonclaw stood behind him and to the side, showing his reverence and loyalty. Their combined packs waited in a half-circle, the two newcomers' packs to fill the other half. The night dragged on, and he knew the other pack leaders desired to make him wait. They wanted to shame him, test his patience. It wouldn't work. Before the night ended, they would have to come, and they would kneel before him. He was the Wolf King. They would pay their respects.

"They are here," said Moonclaw. Redclaw nodded, having detected them as well. They came from upwind, and the scent of their pack rolled over the hill in great waves. His pack yipped and stirred, filled with restless energy. They wanted to see the strength of their leader. No doubt they hoped Murdertongue, Bloodfang, or both, would refuse his rule so they might have their bodies crushed at his feet. Deep down, Redclaw did too. He felt the eyes of everyone upon him, and it made his fur stand on end. Better to lose himself in combat. Better to end his fear than fight it with the tender words humans preferred.

"*Murdertongue!*" cried a hundred voices, and with that the pack came over the hill, loping on all fours. Redclaw stood tall, and despite the tremor in his chest, told himself to remain strong. He would show no fear in the light of the moon. The pack took their places in the circle, leaving only a small gap. Redclaw knew there'd be jostling and biting to make room for Bloodfang. It wouldn't be a true Gathering without it. Instead of joining the circle, Murdertongue stood on the other side of the bone pile from him. He was short for a pack leader, but made up for it with enormous amounts of muscle. Redclaw had met him several times before, watching how he moved. He was slow, but could take a beating. Many scars covered his body, proof of that fact. He was smart, though, and that was where he was truly dangerous. He'd earned his name by talking his pack into slaughtering their previous leader, making way for his accession.

"I have come," Murdertongue said, his voice deep and commanding. "Who is the pup?"

Mooncalw riled at the insult.

"He is Mooncalw. He feasted on Goldteeth's flesh and drank his blood, and now commands his pack."

"Goldteeth, eh? He was a stupid one. I bet he tasted foul."

Mooncalw stepped forward, and he bared his teeth. Redclaw flung an arm in the way, and snarled his disapproval.

"At your place," he said, and Mooncalw dipped his head in obedience. Murdertongue saw this, and sniffed, a reaction signifying either curiosity or contempt. Redclaw figured he had plenty of time to figure out which.

"*Bloodfang!*"

The pack swarmed into the Gathering. Redclaw chilled at the combined sight of the several packs. There were three hundred wolf-men in total, strong and deadly. What human force could be assembled against that might? And they were but the first drop of a downpour.

"I see I have missed no bloodshed," Bloodfang said as he joined them at the pile. He stood near Murdertongue, but far enough away to ensure he showed no allegiance or submission to him. Unlike Murdertongue, he was tall, his spine hardly bearing a shred of curve. His fur was a vibrant red, a rare color for their kind. He grinned at them all, clearly thinking himself funny. Also unlike Murdertongue, Bloodfang was stupid and slow. His pack was on the smaller side, and he ruled through his size alone.

"Plenty of moonlight left," Murdertongue said, and he laughed.

They went through the ritual introductions, with Redclaw going last. His howl was deeper than the others, and he held it for nearly a full minute. The others glared at him, unhappy with being shown up. That earned him the right to speak first, though, and despite his aching lungs and pounding head, he needed his cry to carry across the hills. He stepped onto the pile, walked to its very top, and looked to the crowd.

"Wolves of Murdertongue, wolves of Bloodfang," he cried. "I come not to challenge your leaders. They are strong, and they have earned their right to lead. No, I bring them here, I bring you *all* here, for I have been blessed. The moon shines upon me, and has since my birth. We are not destined for this vile land. We are not meant to eat hyena shit and drink orc piss. We must be free! We must rule a land worthy of ruling!"

"What nonsense do you speak of?" asked Murdertongue. "Say what you mean, so we may all laugh!"

Redclaw narrowed his eyes. Murdertongue was not allowed to speak until he'd finished, and by breaking the rule, he could challenge him now to a contest of strength. But he needed true rule. He didn't want to lead one giant pack. There would be too many, and he would be forced to meet a constant stream of challengers. No, better to let other pack leaders be the targets, to let them all squabble beneath him, with only a few pack leaders carrying the right to challenge his rule. He let the insult pass.

"I say that I know of a way across the river, where the water is shallow and the human boats do not patrol. There is land there, and forest, food and water. Already many of my pack surround it, weakening them, starving them. I ask that you join me! I ask that you come and take what we deserve by right of strength, by right of claw, by right of the moon!"

"And who are you to lead?" asked Murdertongue.

"I am Redclaw, and I will be Wolf King."

The gathered wolf-men went crazy. They howled, nipped at one another, and stomped their feet upon the dirt. Murdertongue's eyes sparkled, but Bloodfang looked ready to explode.

"You would have me kneel to you?" he asked.

"Moonclaw has already, and he is only the first."

"There are a hundred packs," said Murdertongue. "Who are you to claim yourself Wolf King with but a few kneeling to your strength? Not since our creation have we had a Wolf King. You are mighty, Redclaw, but not so mighty as that."

"Not mighty at all!" roared Bloodfang. He stepped onto the pile of bone, his challenge begun. "I will not bow to you. You will bow to me! Tiny wolf, I will take your pack into mine, and they will be stronger for it!"

Murdertongue stayed back, though he could join in at any time. There had been Gatherings in times past where ten or twelve pack leaders descended upon each other at the same time, but the wolf-men had numbered greater then. The orcs had spread across the Wedge, and even the bird-men and the hyena-men had worn away at their numbers. Redclaw crouched, thinking of his law. Wolf may not kill wolf, but Bloodfang was not of his pack, and besides, atop the bone pile they stood upon a tradition greater than Redclaw could dismiss. His mind raced for an answer. Killing Bloodfang gained him little, but leaving him alive would accomplish even less. What chance was there Bloodfang would ever bow his head to him, no matter how many times beaten?

"I do not wish to kill you," he said, carefully watching his opponent's movements.

"But I do!"

Bloodfang launched himself, bones scattering down the pile from where he leapt. Redclaw shifted to the side, so that the bulk of Bloodfang's weight missed. His left arm shot out, grabbing Bloodfang's wrist. A tug, and they rolled atop one another, snarling and biting. Redclaw had timed it well, however, and he ended their roll with his hind legs tearing into Bloodfang's thighs and his claws pinning him to the ground.

"Obey," he cried, his roar thundering across the Gathering.

"No."

Redclaw held him there, and he felt all eyes upon him. Wolf must not kill wolf, he thought. Be King, leader of all packs, not just one. He shoved away and walked to the edge of the bone pile. Behind him, Bloodfang stood, blood dripping down his arms and legs.

"You are weak," Bloodfang snarled. "You are a fool. You are not worthy of any pack, and I will—"

He howled, and his back arced as gore spilled atop the bones from the gaping wound in his belly. Murdertongue held him in a mockery of an embrace, his arms flexed, his claws opening the wound further. Bloodfang struggled, but his strength quickly fled, and his head rolled to one side.

Murdertongue dropped the body and kicked it, sending it tumbling off the pile.

"Will you challenge me now?" Redclaw asked, standing to his full height. His voice, however, was but a whisper, almost a plea in the raucous night.

"Bloodfang's pack is mine," said Murdertongue. "And I still think you are a fool, Redclaw. But perhaps, just perhaps, you may lead us to victory."

He turned to the crowd, lifted his arms to the moon, and then knelt in submission.

"My pack swears obedience," he said, and the entire Gathering erupted into chaos.

Redclaw stood among it, grinning at the crowd. He'd done it. The first step of a hunt was always the hardest. Between Moonclaw and Murdertongue, he had the beginnings of an army. He approached his new comrade, knelt before him, and pressed his nose against his to show their friendship.

"I will reward us with a kingdom," he whispered.

"Pray you do," Murdertongue whispered back.

Standing, Redclaw addressed the crowd, knowing now was the time to solidify his position.

"I am your Wolf King!" he cried. More cheers and howls. "I am leader of packs, now few, but soon to be many. The humans are weak. Their skin is soft, and their minds dull from years of safety. We are the vicious. We are the destroyers. Come the full moon, when our goddess shines and watches our victory, we will cross the river. We will take their land. We will feast upon the flesh of men, women, and children. Imagine the taste of their blood! Imagine their screams in your ears! Few now, but when the Wedge hears, when all know Redclaw stood before the humans and made them tremble, the rest will come. Every pack will kneel. Let your cry reach the stars! All the west will be our prey!"

"You speak the words of the Wolf King," Moonclaw said as he and Murdertongue joined him at the bottom of the bone pile. His fur stood on end, and he clearly felt the excitement of the others. "They cry for blood."

"To the north is a small pack of bird-men," Redclaw said. "They are few, and stay at the edges of my land. Send our wolves upon them. I want them sharp, ready. I want to remind them how poor our food is, tough meat and hollow bones. When we cross the river, I don't want them angry. I want them *hungry.*"

"As you wish...Wolf King," Murdertongue said, leaving to address his pack, now merged with those who had followed Bloodfang. Before he turned, Redclaw saw the faintest hint of a smile on his lips, though what its meaning was, he didn't know, but he felt certain he wouldn't like it if he did.

11

Jerico slept well into the morning, having already given
Jeremy orders for the townsfolk to follow. His rest was
not deep, nor fulfilling, and he rose red-eyed and groggy.
His breakfast was meager, various vegetables fried in animal
fat, with only water from the town's well to wash it down.
After that, he donned his armor, even though he expected
no combat. It would do the people good to see him
prepared, he knew. With his shining platemail and thick
shield, they might think they had a chance to survive while
protected by such a warrior.

Even though it was hopeless. Jerico had seen the pack
gathered that night. But he dared not voice that belief, and
he felt guilty enough thinking it in his heart. Nothing was
hopeless when Ashhur was at his side. But no matter how
often he reminded himself that, he also remembered that
terrible vision of the Citadel cracking and falling, and of the
belief that its fall would mean the end of his order. The end
of him. Was this where the last paladin of Ashhur would
fall, some backwater village lost to the belly of beasts?

"Sorry," Jerico muttered to his god as he stepped from
Jeremy's home. "I'm cranky and stupid. Ignore me."

Darius was already up and about, but he stood in the center of town with Pheus at his side. Wishing nothing to do with the priest, Jerico instead found Daniel and his men guiding the rest of the townsfolk in preparing the defenses.

"You look like shit," Daniel said at his arrival.

"Feel like it, too. How goes the defenses?"

The lieutenant gestured about him. Before three particular buildings the people were digging trenches, boarding up windows, and planting stakes.

"We decided cramming everyone into one single building wasn't feasible, so we settled on three: the inn, the tavern, and Mr. Hangfield's estate. They all have their unique quirks, but we think with enough time we can nail shut the doors and block every window. When they attack, we'll funnel them to a single doorway. If we can negate their numbers advantage, we might stand a chance."

"Where's all the wood coming from?" Jerico asked.

"We've had volunteers. We're tearing down other homes within the wolf-men's circle. Nearly everyone figures they can rebuild if we survive."

"A large if," Jerico muttered.

"The trenches should slow them a little," Daniel said, glaring. "And we'll fill each one with stakes and traps. Figure to build as many as we can before each of the three entrances. All the buildings are within sight of one another, which'll help too. I figure we'll have an archer atop each one, and use 'em to thin the wolves at the doors. Darius also says that priest of his should prove dangerous with open space to cast, so we'll probably stick him atop of Hangfield's."

"As solid a plan as any," Jerico said. "What if they try to starve us out?"

"Well, time's on our side, not theirs right?"

Jerico saw the desperate hope in the lieutenant's eyes, wanting reassurance more than anything.

"Of course," said the paladin. "One of the other towers is bound to notice our absence, if not the traders."

"Right." Daniel looked at the townspeople, and a smile touched his lips. "They're good workers here. If they have any sons to spare, I'll probably try to bring them back with me to Blood Tower. This is the fine stuff true fighters are made of, not those sniveling brats nobles send off in hopes of winning their family honor."

They walked between the three areas, Jerico pointing out gaps in the defenses, plotting locations of more trenches, and correcting angles of the spikes.

"They like to leap," he said. "Remember that. They aren't charging men on foot. Push the tips higher. Make every one of them suffer for jumping too much, or too little."

When he was back at Jeremy's, Jessie came out to greet them. She looked about as bad as Jerico felt, and he felt guilty for not being there to protect her against Yellowscar's attack. He knew it was irrational, but he felt it all the same. After Yellowscar's burial, he'd gone inside to help with the others. The image of that room had haunted his dreams, robbing it of rest. He thought of Darius's anger at giving the creature any form of honorable death. Viewing that carnage, he finally understood.

"Jerico?" she asked, and the paladin bowed politely.

"Yes, Jessie?"

"We, well, some of the others were getting together, and we were hoping you could, you know…"

He smiled even as the selfish part of him wished for anything else in the world.

"Of course," he said. "Where?"

"In the square. The men are about to take a break to eat."

She tried to smile, but it didn't quite take. When she left, Jerico sighed and shook his head.

"She should be worried about which boy to take to the hay-dance, not prayer for friends and family soon to die."

"World ain't fair, nor just," Daniel said.

A vision of the Citadel flashed before his eyes, and then it fell.

"No," said Jerico. "It is not."

"I need a bite to eat myself. Join me when you're done."

Jerico waved him off, then trudged to the square. He took his shield off his back and glanced at its light on the way, feeling childish for needing to do so. He wanted some visual proof of Ashhur's presence, for he felt so exhausted, so trapped. Waiting for him was nearly half the village, men sitting with their wives, their children beside them, the younger ones cuddling on their laps. Some ate, and some drank. When Jerico stepped among them, he felt their presence, their need for reassurance. They were tired, ragged eyed, fighting terror and exhaustion.

"I'm here," Jerico said, for he knew not what else to say. He felt woefully unprepared. His training at the Citadel meant nothing for this. Where were his teachers? Where was their faith that had seemed unshakeable? Before the crowd he felt his neck flush, his hands tremble, and his back go slick with cold sweat. So many of them would die, if not all. What fate awaited them? Would it be Ashhur's graceful hands? Karak's fire in the Abyss? Or only emptiness, a nothing that belied what he knew and believed?

"Thank you for coming," Jessie said, sitting in the front row. Several others echoed similar thoughts.

Jerico bowed his head and closed his eyes. He drowned them out, all of them. Denying his doubt, denying his fear, he spoke to Ashhur as if he were alone. His voice quivered at first, then grew firm. He asked for strength. He asked for forgiveness. He revealed his fear, his uncertainty, and his desperate trust that it would be conquered. Through it all, the people listened.

"**D**o you see them?" Pheus said, watching from afar. His arms crossed, he leaned against a partly disassembled home and frowned at the sight. "Do you see what I warned you of?"

Darius stood beside him, and he keenly felt the shame burn in his chest.

"They are only afraid," he argued. "It will not mean anything beyond today, perhaps tomorrow…"

"The now means everything," Pheus said, willing to hear none of it. "It should be *you* they come to for guidance. It should be *you* who shows them what it means to be strong. When afraid, when facing death, men and women flee to the gods for succor. There will be no lulls to win them back over to you now. No quiet moments of doubt to speak your word. The wolves will come, and fight, and many will die. How many there once sat in your congregation, Darius?"

Taking his greatsword off his back, the dark paladin stared into the black fire that enveloped it.

"Many," he said at last.

"Many?" Pheus sighed. "Even one is too many, and we both know there are far more than one in that gathering. This is your failure. Their lost souls are upon your shoulders for not doing what needed to be done. How tall will you stand before Karak when he asks of this? What will you tell our great lord? I fear what I myself must say. I trusted you, I suppose. Will he accept it? Doubtful. Perhaps we can still acquire some measure of mercy, but only when Jerico dies at our feet. Only when his blood wets your sword and burns in its dark flame..."

Darius sheathed his weapon.

"Enough," he said. "You have made your point. But whoever out there would abandon Karak now in their moments of weakness, they were never true servants of our god. Perhaps we only separate the wheat from the chaff."

Pheus waved a dismissive hand.

"Use platitudes to excuse your weakness if you must, paladin. Those with knowledge will know the truth. I pray you are one of knowledge."

He left. Darius remained, and he listened to Jerico's prayer. It was heartfelt, he knew that for sure. Whether he served a false god or not, he believed it fully. The crowd sang, and cried, and ached for the dead and the soon to be dying. It did not last long, and soon Jerico fell quiet. Some came to talk to him, but most returned to their tasks, shovels and hammers in hand. Jealousy burned in his heart. He had always been the greater speaker, always commanded the greater presence. But it seemed the village almost reveled in Jerico's revealed weakness. It made no sense. How could a trembling of faith affect them more than his iron certainty?

They were only frightened, he told himself. Only tired, scared, and expecting to die. They didn't want laws to live by. They didn't want truths to mold their lives around. They wanted weak grace, a childish promise of safety in the hereafter. Darius frowned, his heart bitter. No Golden Eternity awaited them, only the belly of wolves. He shook his head, knowing he was being cruel. Had he not admitted Jerico his friend a few nights prior? It was only under Pheus's watch that he felt such a failure. What did that mean? Had he fallen from his god's wisdom? For surely the elder priest was closer to Karak than he was...

Doing his best to shove the thoughts from his mind, he approached Jerico and stood before him, feeling strangely awkward.

"A fine job," he said.

"Don't feel like it."

"Trust me on it. Has Daniel informed you of our plan?"

Jerico nodded. "I looked them over. So much of it depends upon the two of us. I don't know if I can do it, Darius."

"You don't have much choice," Darius said, a grim smile on his face. "It'll be just you and me between the wolves and their meal. Neither of us can fail, and we won't, either."

Jerico smacked his shoulder, and for the first time that day, he really smiled.

"Maybe you're right," he said.

"Glad to hear you admit it. Maybe you'll start listening to other things I have to say as well."

It would be the last peaceful night before the wolf-men attacked, and Darius knew he must use it. His muscles ached, for he'd worked side by side with the rest of the village. They'd said little to him, though they showed no animosity or uncomfortable reactions, either. He knew he should be guarding the tavern, but he'd convinced Daniel to send a few of his men over instead under the excuse that he needed to pray, which was no lie.

Darius kept his hand on the hilt of his sword as he approached the thin forest that lay between them and the river. He knew the wolf-men surrounded them, watching for any escape attempts, but he strayed north, not quite reaching the river. He listened for the occasional howls, and he kept his body crouched low. With how bright the moon was, he needed no torch for light. Should he reach the forest, he figured he would be safe for a while. The wolves would expect men to try to flee upon the river, not hide beside it.

Once surrounded by trees, he cleared a space of leaves, and with his hands, tore away the grass until he exposed bare earth. Using his sword, he carved a circle. His throat tightened, and he felt his pulse race. What he was about to do was beyond dangerous. Here he was, a potential disappointment to Karak, ready to enact one of Karak's most sacred rituals. Every motion must be perfect. Every word spoken must be true. Karak was a god of Order, and he would not suffer the presence of one with so much chaos in his heart.

The circle complete, he carved seven runes around it, double-checking each and every one. Satisfied, he thrust his blade into the center, both hands clutching the hilt. Dark fire surrounded it, and he cried out to Karak despite the danger of the wolf-men. The fire burst, and it filled the circle of dirt, though it had nothing to burn. It burned on his faith, he'd been told at the Stronghold, and for it to burn strong, so must he be strong. He repeated prayers to Karak, strengthening the fire. At last he dared make his request known.

"Reveal the fate awaiting me," he whispered. "What will happen if I deny Jerico a death at my hand?"

He stared, not daring to blink, not daring to breathe. In the center of the fire he saw what looked like a dark pebble. It grew, and it seemed like a window to another world, its edges washing over his blade as if it were not there. Within its center he saw the answer to his question.

His heart recoiled, and only his strong will kept his hands closed, his jaw clenched shut.

Jerico stood over him, mace in hand. Blood, Darius's blood, stained its edges. At his feet, Darius saw himself lying there, wounded, beaten, and asking for death.

"No!" he cried, yanking free his blade. Above him thunder rolled, though not a cloud covered the sky. The dark fire continued to burn, traveling up his blade to the hilt. It touched his bare hand, and though it had never harmed him before, today he felt its heat with startling clarity. His skin blackened. His nerves flared with pain. Tears rolled down his face and, unable to withstand the punishment, he dropped his weapon. At the loss of contact, the fire vanished, plain steel landing atop the carpet of leaves. Clutching his blackened hand to his chest, he wept for his weakness.

"Must it be so?" he asked, unable to believe it.

He glanced down at his hand. He expected blistered skin, but instead he saw only the dark hue his flesh had become. He flexed it, and it wasn't tight, nor did it cause him pain. He'd been marked, he knew, permanently branded with his weakness and doubt. A burnt, blackened hand wielding a sword of dark flame. Faith burned both ways, he realized. He was naïve to think otherwise.

"My god asks for your death," Darius said, sheathing his blade. He rolled his hand up in a scrap of cloth, having no desire to look upon it. "And I will obey. You are no friend, Jerico, for what friend would strike me down? I am a paladin, damn it, a paladin of Karak."

Hollow, frightened words, born of pain. He knew it, and he tried to pretend he didn't. Hardening his heart, he returned to the inn and slept. But Karak was not done with him. Throughout the night, Darius had one dream, and it was of himself lying on the ground, Jerico towering over him. They had fought, though he never remembered the beginning, only the end. Every time, it was Jerico who was the mightier paladin, taller, better, and with Darius's blood on his mace.

12

The day passed quiet and uneventful, with most of them sleeping. All but Redclaw. He tossed and turned so much his two pups shifted away, curling their bodies against others of his pack. He didn't blame them, but he was also envious. They didn't understand the momentous occasion before them. They only knew that many were nervous, that their father was quick to anger, and that numerous strangers had come to stay, feasting the night before on orc, goblin, and hyena. Bellies full, they slept while Redclaw watched the steady rise of their chests.

He tilted his head, hiding it from the glare of the sun. Often he wished there were caves about, but knew of none, and the few trees that grew in the Wedge were thin, offering little shade. Shielding his eyes with an arm, he wished for the cool grace of the moon. In it, he felt hidden. In it, he felt like the Wolf King. Under the sun, he was just another wolf-man, doing his best to sleep.

A hand touched his shoulder, and he rolled, growling. An elderly wolf stood over him, and she frowned at the noise he made.

"What is it you want, female?" he asked her.

"Come, and be quiet about it," she said, her voice low. Without an explanation, she turned and began walking toward the river. Grumbling, he glanced at his pups, then followed. Her name was Silver-Ear, though that silver had long since faded to a dull gray. While most elderly fell in battle before reaching Silver's edge, she had been given a special place at the back of every fight, often partaking of fresh blood only after the rest of the pack had obtained victory. She was the shaman of their pack, though rarely did she wield her influence.

The wind howled, and Redclaw wondered if a storm would come. He hoped one would not. The clouds were still a calm white, nearly blotting out the sun. Heavy rains might make the Gihon dangerous, and he didn't want to lose anyone to something as simple as water.

"Where do you take me?" he asked Silver-Ear, having easily caught up with her. Behind them, the pack slowly vanished into the distance.

"You ask what you will soon know," she said. "Is that the patience of a Wolf King?"

"And is it the place of a shaman to command a king?"

Her yellow eyes, dulled and filled with veins, showed a hint of their former youth as she laughed.

"King, pup, or warrior, we of the moon fear none, and speak truth to all. Let us hurry, though, if you so desire. We are almost there."

The ground grew more uneven, and the grass healthier as they neared the river. The clouds deepened, and he felt glad for those on the other side of the Gihon, forced to patrol in the miserable daylight to ensure no one villager escaped, nor any outsiders stumbled upon the situation. At least with the shade they might find rest for their eyes. Silver-Ear led him to the north, stopping twice to track the ground. Sensing they were near their destination, she slowed and began talking, her voice still low.

"I watched your father raise you from a pup," she said. "I know you are a wolf like all others, but you are to be Wolf King. In others' eyes, you must be greater. Your pack listens to me when they must, but I know what I am to them. I am an old gray-fur to help their mates birth their pups, and to crush herbs when sickness makes their noses run and their teeth bleed. But other packs are not like ours. The shamans of the moon hold great sway over their leaders, and there are some who are ruled by their whims. You must convince them as well, and they will not bow to sheer strength."

"Then what will convince them?" he asked.

She led him into a thick copse of trees, and in its center, he saw a cave.

"You pass the rite of the moonless dark."

The cave at first seemed little more than a hole in the ground, but as he looked down he saw it was very deep, the rock twisted and worn. At the bottom it curled inward, and he could see no further.

"What is this rite?" he asked, apprehension swelling in him. He knew he'd wished for a cave, but something about this one seemed dangerous.

"Sit, and I will explain."

She had tied little pouches about her arms with string, the only human form of clothing any of them wore. Opening one, she crushed its leaves and scattered them into a small ring. Chanting ancient words that held no meaning for him, she cast her hands across them. The leaves burst into flame, then quickly petered out, leaving only a heavy trail of smoke rising to the sky.

"Breathe in deep," she ordered. "Goldmoon is foul to eat, but its smoke has purpose."

Its scent was bitter, and he could not focus on its color, for it seemed to change. He felt his head go light and his stomach cramp.

"It will pass," Silver-Ear said. "While the moon sleeps, you will enter a darkness never touched by her light. All shamans must pass a cave like this somewhere in the Wedge, and we guard them carefully. The goldmoon you have breathed in will open your mind to this darkness. You must conquer it, for it will be filled with your fears. Do not turn back, Wolf King. There is but one way, and you must pass through. I will be waiting at the other side."

"What if I do not return?"

She grinned at him, her mouth missing many teeth.

"Then you were never truly our Wolf King. Go into the cave, Redclaw. Go face your fear."

He descended, using the jagged edges of rock as hand and footholds on his way down. The scent of the cave was strong, wet stone, undisturbed earth, and the distant odor of a strange animal's shit. He glanced back at Silver-Ear, but she was gone. His stomach lurched, for it seemed the trees above shivered, and their color grew more and more vivid until at last he did not want to look anymore. Mustering his courage, he crawled into the cave.

Redclaw's eyes were no stranger to darkness, but once he passed the second turn, he found himself in its truest form. No touch of light came here. This was a place the moon never saw. Normally he might use his nose to guide himself, but everywhere was the smell of musty stone. Only the animal shit could guide him, though he still had to inhale deeply. Trying to know where it was strongest was like staring at two blades of grass and trying to determine which was the thicker.

Step after step he went, his back hunched, until there was only room to crawl. His sharp ears heard only the echoes of his claws clicking against the stone. No, that was wrong. He heard other things, but he wanted to believe them only in his imagination. It was a rustling sound, maybe a heavy fluttering...

"I am not afraid," he growled, but immediately wished he hadn't. The sound seemed weak, insignificant compared to the massive amount of stone surrounding him. He was like an ant in the earth, just a lowly ant. His back brushed a column, and he knew at any moment everything could collapse. All his strength, all his dreams of glory, would mean nothing to the rock. Following the thread of scent, he crawled.

Several minutes in, Redclaw saw the first of the visions. Silver-Ear had told him to expect his fears, but this wasn't the combat he had anticipated. Sights hid at the corner of his vision. He heard sounds, but strangely, they did not echo. He heard snarls and growls, and his fur stood on end. Many times it came from straight ahead, but he told himself he would fear nothing. He would back down from no challenge. Random streaks of color flashed before him, never lasting long. He ignored them best he could. His head felt even lighter, and he occasionally shook it and wished he had something to eat. If only he could think clearly, fill his belly with blood and meat to make the sensation go away.

The cavern suddenly opened up before him. His back touched no stone, and a chill wind blew against him. Willing to risk it, he stood, holding an arm above him so he did not bump his head. He touched nothing. Sucking in the cold air, he howled at the top of his lungs, defying the darkness. The noise echoed, seeming to grow with each passing second. His ears ached, but he would not give in. The colors before him merged, taking form, and then he saw the fear the shaman warned him of.

It was his father, Skysight. He had been pack leader, and before his death, commanded a mighty force of four hundred strong. His eyes were a clear blue, and they sparkled with an intelligence most wolf-men could only dream of.

"Why have you come?" asked his father.

"Because I must," he said. "I am Wolf King. I must know no fear."

Skysight laughed.

"Stupid pup. Have you known fear before?"

Ashamed, he nodded.

"And do you know it now?"

"I do."

Another laugh. For a moment Skysight faded, then reemerged. He seemed so bright in the darkness, his body almost entirely white, as if a great moon shone upon him.

"Are you defeated now? Are you no longer Wolf King? What does it matter if you are afraid?"

Redclaw swallowed. His father was dead; he knew this, for he had witnessed his death, along with the near shattering of his pack in a vicious battle against another group of wolves. What was it he spoke to? A spirit? A vision? Or was he hearing only what he wanted to hear?

"It matters," said Redclaw, "for you were never afraid. You were greater than I, yet you were never Wolf King. By what right can I claim it if you never did?"

Skysight shook his head.

"You ask the wrong questions. You make wrong answers. I died, while you lived. I fell to Grassgut, yet you tore out his throat and scattered his pack. How can I be the greater?"

His father shimmered, became a corpse, became bones, and then was gone. Redclaw was once more alone in the cave. Snot ran from his nose, and water leaked from his eyes.

What does it matter if you are afraid?

What indeed? He wished to live. That was all. More than anything, he savored life, and the life of his pups. It gave him purpose. It gave him strength. And when his opponent sought to end his life, more than anything he refused to let them. His fear was from a desire for life, and he knew that, as long as he never succumbed to it, he would be the greater. He was a wolf-man who knew fear when all others knew only bloodlust. Would that be his legacy? Would that understanding grant him the rule he desired?

He crossed the great cavern, following the smell of shit. At the other end, when his claws touched stone, he heard a sound behind him. He turned and saw Goldfoot, his mate. She lay on the ground, her form swarming with shadows. She was not looking at him. Not a sound escaped her lips.

Come to me, he heard, as if the voice came from the center of his head. He almost did. He wanted to lift Goldfoot up, to tell her that her pups had grown strong, that her death in birthing them had granted them life. But Silver-Ear's words echoed in his mind. There was only one way. He could not go back.

"You are not here," he said, the words heavy on his tongue. "You are gone. You are dead. As are you, father. I do not need you. I am mighty. I am Wolf King."

But even the Wolf King knew how small he was when his voice echoed in that cavern. He put his back to the image, shook his head, and then pressed on.

The strange rustling grew stronger as he crawled through another tunnel. Twice he thought he might be stuck, but he sucked in his breath and shifted side to side, refusing to panic. More than anything, he desired the light of day, for even it was better than true darkness. Even its burning fire was better than a night without either. A life without moon and sun was empty; it closed about him, and it made a mockery of his powerful senses. Closer and closer, the rustling. He heard squeaks within it, and by now the smell was potent.

A subtle turn, and then he was there. His eyes winced, and he realized that he could see. Creatures covered the ceiling, and the noise they made was deafening. Bats, he realized, the night birds that flew above them during hunts. The smell of their shit curled his stomach, and breathing its fumes made him dizzy. Turning away, he returned to the large cavern, took in a full, clean breath, and then returned. Holding his breath, he crawled through the bat shit. Redclaw felt their droppings fall upon him, and his anger grew. Was this meant to humble him?

But he could see light, however small. It was nearly blazing to his eyes now, and he followed it quick as he could. One turn, then another, and finally he could hold his breath no more. He let it out slowly, then took in another. The smell was already weaker. A hint of warm air blew across his skin. One bent step, then another, and finally he emerged into the daylight, the exit far larger and surrounded by trees.

Silver-Ear waited for him, and she gestured toward the river.

"Wash yourself," she said. "And drink of the Gihon's water. It will help your head."

He obeyed, surprised that he felt no anger. Silver's eyes held no mockery, no amusement at his state. If anything, she seemed happy to see him. The river's water was cold, but still warmer than the heart of the cave. He dipped his head underneath, then emerged. He drank deeply, then stepped out of the water. Autumn had not reached its strongest, so he would suffer no illness, only mild discomfort at the cold. When he returned to Silver-Ear, she offered him a strip of raw meat from the prior night's feast.

"Eat," she said.

He tore into it, wishing there were more. Once he finished it, he sat before her.

"What did you learn?" she asked.

"That without the moon, without the daylight fire, there is only shit."

Silver-Ear laughed. "Yes, that is true. You are the moon, Redclaw. Even more, you are its King. But remember, there are many others who are the sun. They will frustrate you, anger you, challenge your reign. But they have their purpose. Even ruling over the most frustrating is better than to have no rule at all. Is that all you learned?"

"I know fear, shaman. In this, I am different."

She shook her head.

"All wolf-men know fear, but they hide it with their bloodlust. They do not speak of it, nor admit it to others. That is a lesson we shamans must learn. In hiding their fear, all of our pack will go far. They will kill, shed blood, and challenge mightier foes. But when death comes in the quiet, they still know fear's touch. I have been at the side of many sick, many dying. They know fear, and it is then, having hidden from it their whole lives, they do not know how to face it. But you have, as have we. The other shamans will respect that."

"How will I tell them?"

She stood and gestured for him to lead them back to their pack.

"Tell them you have conquered the moonless night," she said. "Tell them you have overcome the darkness that goes deeper. Invoke my name if you must. You are Wolf King now, in my eyes. I bow to you."

Silver-Ear fell to her knees and flattened her ears. Redclaw took her by the shoulder and lifted her back to her feet.

"All others kneel," he said. "But you must not."

"You are wise, Wolf King," she said, and she smiled.

Once back at the pack, Redclaw returned to his pups. His fur had mostly dried, the sun peeking out from the clouds to bless him with its warmth. The two pups shifted and grumbled, angry at the disturbance. He held them until they stilled, then closed his eyes and curled against them. Sleep came to him only minutes later, and his thoughts did not once stray to the coming battle.

13

With every passing moment, Jerico felt his nerves rise. With every piece of sun that vanished beyond the horizon, he sensed the wolf-men closing in. The gentle warning of Ashhur sounded in the back of his mind, though he had no need of it. He knew the wolves were coming. The town's defenses were prepared. Their fighters, what few they had, were in place. And after sharing with them in prayer, he felt ready to die.

Jerico stood in the doorway of the tavern, leaning against one side. He wore his full set of armor, his shield slung across his arm. It glowed softly, and he took reassurance in its light. Ashhur was with him still. Within, he guarded a scattered remnant of the town's people. Those with children and families were deep in Hangfield's estate. Daniel guarded the entrance with his remaining soldiers. The lieutenant stayed at the front, the rest wielding long, bladed polearms. Across the street stood Darius before the inn, the sick and wounded being cared for by Dolores inside.

Clouds gathered above, stealing away what little light was left. It did not look like rain, and for that Jerico said a word of thanks to Ashhur. The last thing he wanted was to battle in the soaking wet. That, and it would have destroyed the many torches they'd lit throughout the town.

"It'll disturb their vision," Darius had explained. "Blind them to the ditches and pitfalls."

Jerico caught Darius staring at him, and he saluted with his mace. Darius saluted back, his greatsword wreathed in dark flame.

"You all right down there?" shouted Jon, his assigned archer atop the tavern.

"I'll be fine," Jerico shouted back. "You have enough arrows?"

"So long as my aim is true, and you don't leave me more than forty."

Jerico glanced around the corner, saw both Pheus and another archer standing atop the Hangfield home. It was the largest of the three structures, and had the most villagers crammed within. It also had the most openings, though the soldiers had done well boarding them up. Of Daniel's ten soldiers, seven were inside. With them, plus the archer on top, and the dark priest, they might have a chance.

"So they're going to show up soon, right?"

"Getting impatient, Jon?"

From above, he heard the archer chuckle.

"I just don't want to be sitting here for four hours waiting. We're all geared up and ready for a slaughter. Is it so much to ask they show up for it? Besides, this roof ain't the most comfortable."

Jerico swung his mace lazily through the air, feeling similar sentiments. They'd been preparing for two days, and the whole while, he'd felt his patience growing thin. As much as he feared the wolf-men, there would be at least some relief in knowing the pivotal moment had come, that his test of skill had arrived.

In the distance, a wolf howled. It seemed the entire village turned silent, the only noise that of the flickering torches. A second howl joined it, then a third, and in moments a great cacophony rolled through the streets, hundreds of howls of such volume it hurt the ear. Jerico felt his hands grow cold, and his throat tighten.

"Holy shit," Jon muttered.

"We're hoping for a miracle here," Jerico said, shouting to be heard. "Care to keep the blaspheming down a little, eh?"

Despite the terror, Jon laughed.

"Sure thing. I'm better at killing, anyway."

The chorus of howls thinned, the wolf-men no doubt on the charge. Jerico's mace shook in his hand, and he closed his eyes for a moment of prayer. No fear. No cowardice. He thought of the many hiding behind him, with only his shield and mace to keep them safe. His failure meant their death. He would not fail.

He saw the first wolf-man for only a moment before an arrow plunged into its neck. It had stepped around a nearby house, and Darius's archer had spotted it with ease in the torchlight. The thing let out a cry and fell to one knee. A second arrow thunked into its chest, and it lay still. The rest of the pack took up a cry, for they surely smelled the blood spilling across the dirt. Jerico braced himself as scattered groups of wolf-men rushed into view. The first of many spotted him, and it leapt toward him with a deep growl. It tripped along one of the ditches they'd dug and, off-balance, Jerico found it easy prey for his mace. The flanged edges smashed in its skull, and he kicked its body back, just another obstacle for the rest of the pack. Breathing heavily, he swallowed and tried to calm his nerves. The battle of Durham had begun.

His heart leapt into his throat when he heard the sound of tearing wood and breaking doors, but he realized it was only the many abandoned houses. The wolf-men hadn't realized yet that all the survivors had gathered together, and they were busy searching throughout the town. This first assault would be the weakest, the most scattered, and he vowed to build a wall of dead around his door. A group of three wolf-men spotted him, and they charged in unison. Jon unleashed arrow after arrow. Without their armor, they were large, vulnerable targets, and he buried two up to the shaft into the leftmost's chest. The other two vaulted over one ditch, only to crash into the second. Jerico winced, hearing wood snap, and one cried out in pain and did not get up. The other limped toward him, its eyes mad, its leg bleeding from a gaping wound in its thigh.

Jerico stepped into the doorway, knowing the creature would need to duck to enter within, therefore hurting its momentum. It swung its claws, and he blocked with his shield. At their contact, the wolf-man stepped back, yipping in pain. The light swelled on his shield, and taking a step forward, Jerico smashed the wolf in the face with the glowing steel. Blood splattered from its nose, and this time it fell to one knee. Jerico swung, his mace ending its life. The body lay beside the first, another building block for his wall.

An arrow sailed over his head, ending the struggles of the wolf still in the ditch.

"Two to two," Jon cried. "I'm not impressed, paladin."

"Long night left. I got time."

What meager amusement he felt vanished as the rest of the pack appeared. They ran in groups of ten, howling and growling like mad dogs. They numbered in the hundreds, and against such numbers Jerico felt insignificant. His body flooded with adrenaline. This was it. He braced his legs, raised his shield, and prayed the others would endure.

"Fuck," he heard Jon yell. "I don't have enough arrows for *that!*"

The wolves flowed over the ditches and spikes like floodwaters over a dam. Many collapsed, and he heard bones snapping and howls of pain, but they were too few. It only slowed the charge, and only just. Jerico saw two jump at Darius, who cleaved one in half, then engaged the other, his blade blocking claws. Hangfield's was too far to his left to see, so he could only hope they fared well. Arrows sailed from all three rooftops, but it seemed like spitting onto a campfire.

"To me, you monsters!" Jerico cried. "Bring your teeth, your claws, your blood!"

Half the swarm heading for Darius broke off. They flowed over the ditches, accepted Jon's arrows, and slammed against the inn. Jerico braced himself, trusting his shield. The wolf-men slashed at him, but his armor was thick, and he shifted and pushed, refusing to let them pierce through. The power of his shield continued to harm them, and he heard their cries as wolf after wolf could not endure the pain. His arm throbbed, but he ignored it, just as he did the pain in his shoulder. Careful, methodical, he shoved with his shield, swung his mace in the brief opening, and then stepped back in retreat. Nearly every time, his mace drew blood. Too many of them pressed together, Jerico knew, unable to dodge or parry. They expected to bury him with sheer mass and muscle. They were wrong.

Piles of bodies built before him, until the wolf-men had to climb over. That was when he made a rare attack, wading into his opponents, his shield and mace slamming with brutal fury. He would not fail. He would not let them die. His shield struck a wolf in the chest, and as it staggered back, he cracked its skull from the top, dropping it into a heap before him. Standing atop it, he leapt at the next, blocking its desperate slash with his shield. Its other arm made it past, and it cut a deep groove in his breastplate. No blood, though the same could not be said for Jerico's counter. He broke its jaw, swung again, and blasted an eye out from its socket. The wolf-man collapsed, and for the moment, Jerico could see out his door to the space between their buildings.

He wished he couldn't. More wolves, scores of them. He heard wood tearing, and he saw many pulling at the boards to various windows. Once they made it in, they could attack from multiple directions. If that happened…

"Cowards!" he screamed. Much as his body ached, much as he desired the reprieve, he knew the wolf-men needed to be kept wild with anger, unable to think, unable to realize the disadvantage they faced when challenging him in the doorway. He struggled to find breath to even cry out, but still he did. "Will you hide? Will you run? I am here, yet you play the coward and try for women and children?"

"You will die, human!" one cried, and several took up the cry.

"Blood," they shouted. "Blood from the humans!"

An arrow sailed into the throat of the first, but this time, there was no bragging from Jon, no jokes.

"Get him," shouted one of the wolf-men. Jerico felt his blood run cold, but he could do nothing. Several charged him, while others climbed the walls. Praying for the best, Jerico braced his legs once more, smacked his shield with his mace, and met the yellow gaze of his foe. Shield raised, he could only hope to endure for a time, until the wolves finally broke him down, split his armor, and had their feast.

The first wave was the easiest. Daniel stood in the center, his sword at ready. To his side and his back, his trusted soldiers held polearms. They were a wall of thorns and spears, and the first wolf that leapt at them found out the hard way. Blades pierced its body in three places, it fell to the ground, shoved away by the soldiers. The next two met similar fates, and Daniel dared to hope. Then the entirety of the attacking pack arrived, and he realized how foolish he had been. They tripped into ditches, they impaled themselves on the spikes, and still they came.

"Brace!" he commanded, and the men did. Three wolf-men leapt at once, slamming onto the ends of their weapons as if they desired death. Daniel swung his sword, lopping the head off one and piercing another through the heart. They could not shove them aside, though, for the wolves were a river, and it flowed against them in a constant stream of muscle, claws, and howling. Daniel stood in the center of it all, trusting his men to keep him from being overwhelmed. For a moment he felt like the young man he had been, his sword a part of himself, a shining death that cut through defenses and showered the ground with gore.

And then the priest made his presence known. A sound like thunder rolled across them, and lightning struck the earth, its center a deep black. A crater sunk at its impact, and several wolves crumpled, their innards blackened. Daniel cheered at the raw display of power. The strange priest certainly had his uses. Renewed, he let out a cry and cut down his attackers.

But Daniel's strength soon failed him, and despite the spears, wolf-men twisted and slashed undeterred. Claws raked across his forehead. Blood ran across his eyes, and blinded, he fell back. His men closed the gap instantly, the entryway of the house filled with the sound of battle. Collapsing against a wall, he sat there as someone wiped away the blood and pressed a heavy cloth against his wound.

"It is not lethal," Jeremy said, apparently his nurse.

"Course not," Daniel muttered. "Take more than a scratch to bring an old bull like me down."

He was blustering, of course. His head throbbed in agony, and he felt like his breath would never come back to him. Still, he forced himself to a stand. Another soldier fell back, blood gushing from his torn throat. Daniel tried to take his place, but his men would not let him.

"Rest," Gregory said, commanding the defense. "Take your place when you must."

"Fine," Daniel said, turning to Jeremy. "Tie this, will you?"

Jeremy knotted the cloth behind his head, pulling it so tight he thought his skull was going to explode. He gritted his teeth and endured the pain. As he picked up his sword, he heard screams from further in the house.

"The windows?" he asked.

"Men guard them," Jeremy said. "But yes, I fear so."

"Hold the door," Daniel shouted to his men. "By the gods, we'll make legends of ourselves tonight, if we must!"

He and Jeremy hurried down the hall, following the sound of screams. In the first bedroom, they found a single farmer thrusting a pitchfork into a gap in the window, half the boards covering it torn loose. The farmer's wife and children huddled beside the door, sobbing. Two wolf-men batted at the pitchfork and dug at the boards like wild animals.

"Stand firm!" Daniel shouted, joining the farmer. His sword thrust into the gap, and he smiled with grim satisfaction at the resistance he felt, knowing his blade pierced chest or belly. He pulled back, thrust again, and now emboldened, the farmer stabbed with his pitchfork, giving no more ground. The first fell dead, but it was replaced by another. Arms reached into the room, seeking anything to grab hold of with their sharp claws. Daniel swung, the farmer stabbed, and they built their own pile of dead at the window.

All at once, the assault stopped.

"Brace your pitchfork," Daniel said, gasping for breath. "Don't you run on me, you hear? You stand here, stand tall, and keep that fucking thing pointed at the window."

The man nodded. His eyes were wide, his skin pale. He was a hair's width away from running. It didn't matter that there was no safety anywhere in the village. All he wanted was away from the wolves, Daniel knew, to where he didn't have to see their hungry eyes, their shining teeth, and their wicked claws. Daniel stood beside him, aimed his blood-soaked blade at the window, and again ordered him to stand firm.

"Here they come," he said, seeing yellow glinting in the torchlight. The wolf-men, tired of trying to push through, had gained some distance so they could run. Leaping into the window, they crashed through the boards, the first one impaling itself on the farmer's pitchfork. The man let out a cry, his bladder let go, but he did not run. Daniel felt proud, and he refused to let the wolves gain entry. He cut down the next, then stepped closer, calling for the farmer to join his side.

"Jeremy!" he cried. "Get men in here. Beds, boards, anything to block this damn window!"

Another thunderclap shook the house, and Daniel hoped the priest had killed twenty of the sons of bitches overrunning the village. Through the window, he saw the wolf-men gathering, preparing another leap. Three lay dead on the floor of the room, and he could do nothing to remove them. Seeing the pack, seeing their numbers, he could not blame the farmer's desire to run. They were endless, and he was old, and tired. The night, however, was still young.

"You run, I cut you down," he said to the farmer. "And I run, you better do the same damn thing to me."

Blade and pitchfork lifted, they drank in the blood of wolves as the next charge came.

><><

Darius's sword cleaved through his foes, and in the chaos of combat, he felt like an exultant beacon of order. Above him his archer, Letts, was emptying his quiver while shouting warnings.

"Two at right!" Letts cried, firing an arrow off in that direction. Two wolf-men, hoping to surprise him, curled about the inn and leapt. Darius stepped into the attack, ducking under the first's claws and swinging. His greatsword cut the damned creature in half, spilling its gore across the dirt. The second slammed into him and they rolled. Claws scraped his armor, and teeth sank into the gorget protecting his throat.

"Get off me, you bastard!" Darius cried. He pressed his blackened hand against its breast. All his anger poured through, a powerful blow made stronger by his faith in Karak. The wolf-man flew back, smoke billowing from a hole in its chest. Darius stood, having little time to prepare before three more assaulted him. Letts took down one, then swore.

"Bad dog, down!"

Wolf-men were climbing the sides of the building, but there was nothing Darius could do but hope Letts handled it himself. The first rammed into him, but Darius held firm, piercing its heart with his blade. He tore it out the side, cutting off the head of a second. Bone and muscle were like wheat to Darius's mighty scythe, and he felt himself the reaper. The third wolf scored a hit against his side, his claws sinking in through a gap in his armor. He sliced off its hand at the wrist for such insolence, then opened its throat.

Above him, Letts screamed.

"Letts?" Darius asked as he caught his breath. "Letts!"

The archer's body sailed over his head and landed in a heap. He spun, saw wolves crawling across the roof, tearing at the shingles. Already he saw gaps opening up. Darius thought of Dolores inside, of the many wounded. He turned back, and already a group of five were preparing to charge. He couldn't save them. Guilt clawed at his throat, but what could he do? In the distance, he saw the soldiers handling the wolves at Hangfield's, but only because the priest continually cursed and disrupted the assaults. But Jerico...

The paladin of Ashhur was surrounded by foes, and the best he could do was stand firm with his shield and hope to endure. In minutes, he'd be buried.

"I'm sorry," Darius whispered to the inn. To Karak or Ashhur they'd go. There was no hope left for them. Abandoning his post, he slashed through the wolf-men, ran across open ground, and lunged into the group gathering around Jerico. He kept his back to the inn, not wanting to see the wolf-men enter, not wanting to hear the screams of the dying, imagine Dolores torn to pieces...

"At my side!" Jerico ordered, and Darius obeyed. They linked up, two paladins side by side, and faced the wolf horde.

"Your charges," Jerico asked.

"I could not save them."

There was no judgment in Jerico's eyes, only sadness mixed with determination.

"You did all you could. Stand with me."

The wolves leapt, driven mad by the stench of blood and carnage. Bodies lay in great stacks, the wolf-men needing to climb over many just to make an attack. Like ancient heroes of old, the two paladins held firm. Those who attacked found only Jerico's glowing shield awaiting them. Those who fled felt the black blade of Darius pierce their backs.

Jerico took up song as he fought, a jaunty tune Darius had heard in many taverns. He laughed aloud as he realized its title: The Wolf and the Maiden. One line amused him to no end, and he sang along as his sword whirled.

"And down, down, down came the woodsman's axe, down, down, down!"

How well the wolves understood their song, Darius didn't know, but it seemed to infuriate them to no end. On and on they came, leaping over ditches filled with their dead, crawling over the walls of their bodies. He couldn't think of how many he killed. The number was lost to him. Twenty? Thirty? His arms ached. Scratches lined his face and neck. The taste of blood remained permanent on his tongue. But he sang along with Jerico all the same, until a great cry pierced the noise. Appearing none too pleased, the wolf-men backed away, growling amongst themselves.

"What's going on?" Darius asked.

"I don't know. Jon, you still alive?"

The archer waved an arm over the top of the roof.

"You guys are scaring the shit out of me," said Jon. "Dear gods, how many did you kill?"

Darius glanced at the dead and shrugged.

"A lot."

They heard shouts, and a large commotion spread to the center. It was then they saw Redclaw lording over the pack, giving orders, commanding with his howls. Their eyes locked, and Darius felt chills flow through his blood. The wolf was unafraid, unimpressed with their stand.

"Their leader," Jerico whispered.

"If he dies, we might break their spirit."

The wolves about them seemed small by comparison to that center group, and Darius realized they had fought the weakest, the scouts and runners. In a group of near a hundred were the true elites, the muscle of the wolf pack. Above them Redclaw towered, and Darius had no desire to face him.

"We did well," he said. "Let us die knowing that."

Jerico laughed.

"You can die, if you like. We're not done yet, Darius. We'll pat our backs in the morning, with breath still in our lungs."

"Amen," said Jon from the roof.

Redclaw stepped forward, and the three fell silent, for the leader began to speak.

Night of Wolves

14

If all humans were this strong, Redclaw knew the wolves of the Wedge could never claim a land of their own. He surveyed the damage, strangely unafraid. The loss of life felt distant to him, for many were not of his own pack. Even being in human lands felt unreal, but at the same time, a fulfilled destiny. No matter how many died, he would take this village, and the next, until his entire race had itself a proud nation. But these villagers were strong, and though they had killed many breaking into one of their buildings, still the two defended structures remained.

Redclaw had watched the fight for a time, seeing both defenders. The larger building, the one with many boarded windows, was guarded by human men that he had seen and fought before. They wore metal for skin, and gathered together for strength. Their long blades kept his wolves at bay, for they could not swarm them like they could on open ground. But they were still weak, and he could see their movements slowing. In time they would fall, and all within would die. Only the strange man on their roof appeared truly dangerous, wielding magics that confounded reason. The attacks had slowed, though, the man garbed in black possibly lacking the strength to continue.

But these two…

"What are they?" he asked Murdertongue, hoping the intelligent wolf might know.

"I do not know," Murdertongue replied. "Surely they are men, like any other."

Redclaw shook his head. The shield of one glowed with a blue light painful to look upon, while the other swung a massive sword that burned with black fire. They held their ground against his pack, unafraid. They even sung to them in mockery! Side by side, they seemed unbreakable. They were champions of the human race, he realized, the ones Yellowscar had spoken of. No wonder he had lost so many! They were the best, the strongest, the bravest. Calling his pack together, he ordered a stop to the attack. Reluctantly they returned to him.

"Moonclaw, take twenty to the back of the house," he said, pointing to the place guarded by the soldiers. "Murdertongue, keep them busy at the front."

"What of them?" Moonclaw asked, gesturing to the human champions.

"Five of you, stay with me," he ordered. "I will remain here. Against all our numbers, the others cannot hope to live. Let the champions brave the open ground if they wish to save them. Let them face me in combat! We will not play their game. We will not crouch under tiny roofs."

Orders given, he let out a cry, sending them into motion. Patience, he told himself. He had been a fool in giving the humans warning. He'd wanted greater numbers, and a chance for them all to feast. He'd expected the humans to be hungry, tired, but instead they'd built trenches and placed sharpened poles in all directions. For the next attack, he would need to use speed and surprise. If they had not been gathered in those buildings, if they had not prepared their defenses, already his packs would be feasting on their flesh.

With the five at his back, he approached the two humans.

"Champions, I am Redclaw, Wolf King of the Wedge. Who are you to defy me?"

"Darius Wolf Slayer," said the man with the black blade.

"And you can call me Jerico Wolf Smacker."

"You do not amuse me. Do you think we will not suck the marrow from your bones before the moon sets?"

They both shrugged.

"I see far more of your dead than mine," Darius said.

Redclaw snarled. They were certainly right about that.

"You are tired," he said. "And your games are nothing. My wolves descend upon this village, and a scattered few will not stop us. Then we will come for you. We will tear the wood from these walls. We will rip the roof from its base. There is no stopping us."

"Sure there is."

Redclaw looked up to see a third man on the roof, a bow in hand. An arrow shot from the string, and it thudded into the eye of the wolf-man beside him. Redclaw snarled, and he caught the dying body of his fellow wolf-kin.

"Last shot," said the archer. "Figured I'd make it a good one. Shame I missed. Was hoping for your throat, Redclaw."

Redclaw felt his blood boil as he set the body down. He glanced at the archer, an unarmed man with a cowardly weapon. More than anything, he felt a desire to feel his bones crunch between his teeth, and he let it overwhelm his fear at realizing death had been so close, just the slightest correction in flight by the archer.

"Keep them here," he ordered the remaining four. "Do not let them escape."

He bolted to one side, running on all fours. The sudden exertion felt wonderful to his muscles. All night, he'd stayed back from the fight, behaving as he thought a king should. But that was the way of human kings, perhaps. He should have been in the fray long before. How many wolves might he have spared by slaughtering the defenders? He was the strongest, the fastest. He should have acted like it.

Climbing the building was simple, the wood providing easy grip for his claws. In moments he was on top. The archer, instead of trying to flee, surprised him by lunging with his dagger. Redclaw bit at it, catching the blade in his teeth. A vicious jerk and the weapon went flying. This time the archer did run, heading toward where the two champions stood. A kick of his legs and he flew across the roof, his claws sinking into the man's back. He twisted and slashed, relishing the warm flow that spilled across his hands. His teeth sank into the man's neck, opening veins. Blood poured across his tongue, and he drank it eagerly. Fulfilling his desire, he tore free the man's collarbone and crunched it in his teeth. The resulting ecstasy flooded his primal mind.

Hurling the body to the ground, he stood above the champions, reared back, and let his roar ascend to the heavens, let the moon hear his exaltation of the most basic desires of his race.

His sharp ears sensed a shift in the battle, and he glanced to where the combat had begun anew. The defenders at the front had retreated within, whether killed or falling back, he could not yet tell. The two men below him noticed as well, and he caught them staring at the great wave of wolf-men flowing into the building.

"Is it not as I said?" he told them, hoping to break their spirit. "All within will die, and then we will come for you."

The men looked to one another, and it seemed as if they were somehow communicating. When they reacted, it was far from what Redclaw expected. The two broke for the building, leaving their own place unguarded. Baffled, Redclaw stood and watched. The four wolf-men met them in battle, and in open ground they stood a better chance, but only a little. The black blade looped about, and they had no defense against it. Severed claws struck the ground, followed by arms, followed by heads. The glowing shield shifted back and forth, protecting Darius as well as its wielder. Redclaw couldn't believe the sight. These were his best, his finest, and mere humans were tearing them apart. Had they, too, been raised in a lifetime of battle? Was their training so great that even the wolf's speed and strength could be overcome?

Redclaw had terribly underestimated his opponents. There would be more like this, he realized. How many? Ten? A hundred? A thousand? His knowledge of humans was limited to the few he'd slain. Their flesh was soft. Their armor was a lie, metal twisted and shaped to protect their vulnerable bodies. They wielded heavy weapons that could only wish to be as fast as their claws. What was this? What magic gave their shield and sword power? What lunacy allowed the man in the black robe to command dark lightning, and to knock back his wolf-men as if they were playthings?

Still, he could not hesitate further. He could not allow fear to hold him back. He leapt from the roof, for the way into the building was clear. If the champions wanted to leave the rest unprotected, so be it. But as the last of the four went down, the one with the shield, Jerico, rushed back. His mace struck at him before he had even landed from his jump. Redclaw pushed aside the blow, then rammed his head forward, striking the metal on the man's chest. As he fell back, Redclaw looked to the other. Darius charged the rest of his pack, slicing through several before they realized a foe had come upon them from behind.

"He will die, buried beneath my brethren," Redclaw said.

"Perhaps," said Jerico. "But how many of your brethren will he take with him?"

"You are tired. I see it. Your shoulders sag, and your breath is heavy."

Jerico grinned at him.

"And you are afraid. I see the terror hidden in your yellow eyes. We'll see who breaks first."

Redclaw feinted a slash with his left arm, then curled in with his right, charging at the same time. His claws raked against armor, but he felt the metal give, felt it crunch inward against the weak flesh. The champion's mace swung, but he shifted his body enough so it only glanced off his shoulder. Two more slashes scraped against the chestplate, and then the shield was in the way. At its touch he felt pain spike up his arms, and he retreated. They faced one another, blood dripping down Redclaw's shoulder, Jerico wincing and glancing at his chest.

"Your armor does not hide your bleeding," Redclaw said.

"Neither does your fur."

Redclaw rushed again. He bit and slashed, using every shred of strength to break the champion down. Yet each blow upon the shield felt like he was trying to crush the very earth itself. His speed was enough that Jerico could scarcely hope to retaliate, but even so, his frustration mounted. The flanged edges cut him, shallow wounds that mounted and soaked his fur with his blood. The champion bled as well, from his wrist, his face, his neck. Nothing deep. Nothing fatal. Roaring, he tried to bury Jerico under his charge, but again the man stood firm and held him back.

"You must fall!" Redclaw cried. "This is my fate. This is my kingdom! I have conquered the faceless dark! I am Wolf King!"

"And I'm Jerico, and I don't care."

Redclaw could no longer contain his fury. He wanted this man beaten, bloodied, and shown how pathetic he was. He fought to protect those within, so it was those he would eat while he watched. Their fight had them circling each other many times, and with the human's exhaustion, he could not keep himself positioned perfectly. Redclaw feinted, then dove for the door.

"No!" he heard Jerico scream. It was music to his ears.

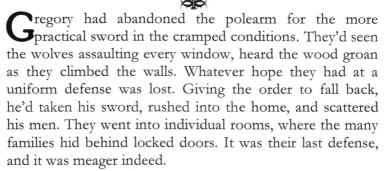

Gregory had abandoned the polearm for the more practical sword in the cramped conditions. They'd seen the wolves assaulting every window, heard the wood groan as they climbed the walls. Whatever hope they had at a uniform defense was lost. Giving the order to fall back, he'd taken his sword, rushed into the home, and scattered his men. They went into individual rooms, where the many families hid behind locked doors. It was their last defense, and it was meager indeed.

Slamming the door shut behind him, Gregory turned and surveyed his surroundings. He was with Jeremy, his daughter, and another family of four. Jeremy held a shortsword, and he faced him with terror in his eyes.

"The door," he said, as if that should explain everything.

"Overwhelmed," Gregory said, pointing at the window. "You stand there and guard it with your life. Thrust through the cracks, but don't let them grab hold."

Gregory faced the door, locked it, and pushed a dresser in the way. As the first wolf-man slammed into it from the other side, he wondered how in the world he had ended up in such a predicament. He'd been considered a promising recruit for the Mordan army, but then his father had slighted king Baedan. As a way of humiliating him, he'd sent Gregory to the wall of towers, where the greatest honor he could have expected was killing a few brave orcs who crossed the river. Or so he'd thought. Should he survive, they'd sing praises of the defense of this village. At least, he'd pay a damn bard to compose one and sing it a few times. Only seemed right.

The lock broke, and he wasn't surprised in the slightest. The wolves were strong, and he feared he would be a poor match against them in close quarters. Still, he wasn't going down without a fight. The door pushed back as two more wolves joined in, knocking the dresser further with each wave. Gregory stabbed into the opening, scoring wounds each time. The wolf-men appeared oblivious to any danger. They might have gotten inside uninjured if they were careful, but that seemed counter to their nature. Everything was brutal, rushed, seeking to overwhelm an opponent with sheer strength and speed regardless of injuries. That tactic had failed in the tight spaces of the estate's doorway, facing a coordinated defense, but one on one...

He stabbed with renewed vigor. By the gods, he wasn't going down without a pile of bodies at his feet! Two different yelps greeted his effort, and then the door blasted open. Desperately wishing he had a shield, Gregory met the advance. He cut one down, and he used its falling body to stall the other. His sword could cut and wound, but the wolf-men lunged with such energy that even killing one would not prevent it from crashing into him. The two families screamed, and Gregory tried to make his stand.

"Gregory!" Jeremy shouted. A wolf-man grabbed hold of Gregory's arm, and he screamed as he felt muscle tear. He stabbed his sword up to the hilt in the wolf-man's chest, and then spared a glance behind. Something was crashing through the broken boards on the window. Jeremy fell back. It was no wolf-man. Darius hit the floor, spun, and swung his sword in an upward arc. A chasing wolf-man howled, its body cut in two. Gore splattered the floor, and the two families screamed.

"Take the window!" Darius ordered, physically grabbing him and flinging him behind. His burning blade made quick work of one wolf-man, and it kept a second at bay. Gregory joined Jeremy at the window, and when the first tried to climb through, they stabbed it with their swords, knocking it back. It seemed few were there to take advantage of the opening, not with the front doors unguarded.

"There's too many!" Gregory shouted, leaving the window to join Darius's side.

"Really? I never noticed!"

Darius braced with his back foot as the wolf-man lost patience and charged, impaling itself on the burning blade. The dark paladin kicked the body off in time to battle a second, this one smaller, faster. Claws ripped off the armor from his shoulder, tearing the leather strap in two. Blood ran, but Darius fought on, his scream drowned out by that of the wolf as he hacked through its collarbone and into its chest.

They heard cries from the other rooms, and Gregory could only imagine how the rest of their men fared. Where was Daniel? Jon? Letts? Was the priest dead, or had he simply exhausted his repertoire of spells? And what of Jerico? Still the wolves rushed through the hallways, seeming endless in number. Would they fight all night, never to know victory?

"Gregory?" Darius asked, standing before the door with his shoulders slumped, gasping in air during a momentary reprieve.

"Yeah?"

"Is it me, or am I hearing trumpets?"

Gregory paused, and sure enough, he heard the same brass sound.

"Yes," he answered.

"Good," Darius said, taking up his sword as another wolf-man turned the corner and rushed for him. "I was worried I'd lost so much blood I'd begun hearing things."

15

Jerico didn't want to imagine the carnage within. He didn't want to face the failure of his poor positioning, of letting the self-proclaimed Wolf King through. But he went inside anyway.

"Ashhur damn you to the Abyss," he whispered. Redclaw had had only a moment's time, but he'd used it well to suit his desire. Blood splattered the walls. People screamed, and men and women lay dying on the floor. The wolf-man tore through those that fled, trying to hurry up the stairs or to the exit. Jerico rushed in, ashamed of his pause. There was no time to take in his surroundings, no time to dwell on his failure. Only one thing mattered: Redclaw's death.

"Do you hear their wails?" Redclaw asked, whirling to face him, a torn arm hanging limp in his grip.

"I do." He flung his mace, the flanged edges striking the Wolf King across the side of his face. "And I hear yours, too."

He charged, shield leading. Only a fool would consider him unarmed without his mace. The glowing surface slammed into the wolf-man, its holy light burning. Redclaw howled, and despite his training, Jerico felt joy in the sound.

At least ten lay dead or dying because of the creature. Hopefully Ashhur would forgive him for taking delight in Redclaw's death. He punched with his gauntlet, braced his knees, and then lunged again. His shield struck the Wolf King's chest, accompanied by a flash of light.

"I am no pup!" Redclaw roared. Despite the pain from its contact, he slashed the shield anyway, shoving it back and denting its surface. "I am no fool! You will die, human. We will be free, free to roam, free to feast! The western lands belong to your kind no longer!"

"The blood on your face says otherwise."

Redclaw snarled, and Jerico ducked underneath the desperate strike. Bending down, he grabbed his mace, spun, and struck the wolf-man on the underside of his chin. The blow rocked him to his heels, and Jerico followed it up with a shield to the face. Blood splattered across the metal of his armor. The paladin couldn't deny the immense satisfaction. So many dead. So many dying.

"We are too many," Redclaw said, but his voice was nearly a whimper. He staggered away, his weight leaning against a wall. One eye had swollen shut from the thrown mace, and blood dripped from his nose and teeth.

"I know," Jerico said, not worried about the remaining few who heard him. "But we stood strong anyway, wolf. You know we beat you. You'll die knowing it, as I'll die knowing we crushed your pack. This land is ours. Go back to the Wedge."

Redclaw tensed, Jerico braced his shield, but then the wolf-man tore to the side, rushing past him and out the door. The paladin thought to call him a coward, but insulting a fleeing creature seemed both petty and pointless. It'd be like calling a dog a dog and thinking it'd care. His armor feeling like it weighed a thousand pounds, he staggered back to the door. The last of his adrenaline was fading, Ashhur's lent strength seeming to fade. He'd faced their best, and won. At least he knew that.

Stepping out from the tavern, he looked to Hangfield's. He expected it destroyed, to hear the cries of the dying, or even worse, the sound of feasting. Instead, the creatures appeared in disarray. Wolf-men were looking about, and many rushed from the main door. Before Jerico could begin to wonder why, he heard the heavy sound of a trumpet, shockingly close. Glancing the other way, he saw a squad of twenty soldiers on foot rushing toward the wolves, armor shining and swords raised high. An older man led them, his hair and beard gray, but his battle-cry sounded youthful enough. Jerico laughed and wondered if he'd somehow lost his mind.

The soldiers crashed into the back ranks of the wolves, who clearly lacked any leadership. Keeping tight battle lines, the humans waded through them, pressing toward the house. Jerico took up his shield and joined in. The wolf-men had already suffered tremendous casualties, and against the reinforcements, however few, they were unprepared. Jerico heard the soldiers singing as they fought, and he sang along. His mace struck once, twice, bringing down a wolf-man, and then his shield led him on, smashing aside two more to link up with the soldiers.

"What miracle brought you here?" he asked as the wolf-men surrounded them, forming a loose perimeter that was unable to punch through their shields.

"If it is a miracle, it's a damn poor one," shouted the older man. "Because all you got was me, paladin."

"I'll gladly take it," Jerico laughed. With him in the lead, he broke the wolf's line, using his shield to fend off two attackers hoping to bury him with their weight. The way to the house clear, they rushed in, cutting down a few stragglers trying to flee. Inside, he found Darius, who saluted with his gore-coated blade. It seemed even the dark fire was struggling to burn away all the blood.

"Friends of yours?" Darius asked him, gesturing to the soldiers.

"Friends of mine," Gregory said, stepping past. "Robert, you old bastard!"

The older man hugged him, then gestured about.

"An interesting fortress."

"It did its job," said Daniel, emerging from one of the rooms. He walked with a limp, and blood covered his left side, but he looked like he'd live another twenty years easy. "Why in blazes are you here?"

Robert looked back to his men, who had formed a wedge and begun chasing after the wolf-men, who had taken flight outside.

"Looks like we'll miss the rest of the fun," he said.

"Good. Tired enough just making my way here. The young can go do the chasing."

Jerico leaned against the wall and, finally able to relax, he felt a massive weight leave his shoulders. They'd lived. Somehow, someway, they'd lived.

"What brought you here?" Gregory asked.

"Believe it or not, King Baedan sent us a few more recruits. I kept 'em for myself, but figured I'd escort some of my more veteran men down to Tower Violet. I planned to keep going, pay respects to the paladins at the Citadel for aiding us, but then we ran across some traders two days back. Claimed wolf-men assaulted their boat when they tried sailing south past Durham. We rode the river all night and day to reach you, and by the looks of it, we weren't that terribly needed. Goddamn, Daniel, I swear we walked through the town on the bodies of wolves!"

"The King sent us men?" Daniel asked when the story was told. "Truly?"

Sir Robert laughed, and he winked at Jerico.

"Aye, he did. So maybe there is a miracle in all this, eh, paladin?"

"Come," Darius said, hefting his sword onto his shoulder. "Let's take final count of all this mess."

He exited, and Jerico followed.

"Good to see you survived," Jerico said.

"I'm glad I did, too. Had to crash in through a window. Thank Karak the wolves softened it up for me first."

Jerico laughed and elbowed the dark paladin. Darius grinned.

"Fine. Glad to see you lived as well. You got that monster, I take it?"

"He fled," said Jerico, a bit of his smile fading. "And he made it inside the tavern. So many..."

They stopped in the center of the town, which appeared to be the spot of a great slaughter given how many corpses lay strewn about, all of them wolf-men. Someone called out Darius's name, and they both turned to see Pheus approaching. Jerico felt his stomach tighten, but he did his best to ignore it. They'd survived against terrible odds, and while many had died, many had also lived. He would bear no ill will against the troubling priest, given how much he had aided their struggle.

"Darius," said the priest. "The battle is done, and the wolf-men beaten."

"You state the obvious," Darius said, but his mood soured. Jerico frowned, wondering what bothered his friend so.

"With the threat over, your last excuse is gone. Will you do what must be done?"

Darius approached the priest, and he leaned close as if to whisper an answer, but Pheus pushed him back.

"No secrets," he said. "No whispers, no silence. Do you have the courage, or do you not?"

"Darius?" Jerico asked, wondering what was going on, and not liking the cold feeling traveling up his neck.

"This is not what Karak wants," Darius insisted.

"You are to tell me what Karak wants?" the priest asked. He looked flabbergasted. "You, a child in armor, a weakling in our god's eyes, would tell me his will? Step aside, paladin. You shame your name, and all your brethren, with such cowardice."

Eyes downcast, Darius stepped back. Pheus glared at Jerico, and shadows danced around his fingers, swelling with power. Reluctantly Jerico lifted his shield, his fingers wrapping about the mace clipped to his belt.

"What nonsense is this?" he asked, wishing for any other explanation.

"Your friends are dead, paladin of Ashhur. Your kind will soon be a fading memory from this world. Go to the Abyss with my blessing."

Darius's sword slashed out, resting against the pale flesh of Pheus's throat.

"No," said the dark paladin.

The priest's whole body trembled with rage.

"What are you doing?" he asked.

Darius shook his head. He still looked troubled, but a change had come over him. He stood tall, and his words were firm, proud.

"You are not the will of our god. Because of Jerico, these people survived. I refuse to believe Karak would honor such bravery with death and betrayal. The wolf-men represent the chaos of this world, not him. Speak another word of that spell, and I will silence you forever."

"You would threaten a priest of Karak? You would betray your own order?"

"I betray no one, Pheus. Go on your way."

Pheus's eyes flickered between them. Decision made, he relaxed his arms, and the shadows faded away from his hands.

"The Stronghold will hear of this," he said.

"I know."

"They will not look kindly upon you."

Darius sighed.

"I know."

The priest shook the dust from his sandals, turned, and walked west. Darius watched him go as Jerico stood there, confused beyond all measure on how to feel. His friend saw this and sighed, finally tearing his gaze away from the retreating priest.

"We must talk," he said.

"After them," Jerico said, pointing to where the many families were exiting Hangfield's, seeking friends and loved ones from the other two places they'd defended. "There's a lot of grief, a lot of death. Let us perform our role."

Darius stabbed his sword into the dirt.

"So be it."

When the prayers were done, and every possible word of consolation had passed from Jerico's lips, he retreated beyond the center of town and built a fire. He knew its light would guide Darius there, and sure enough, the paladin arrived not long after.

"Two thirds dead," Darius said, shaking his head as he sat. "Some victory."

"They'll rebuild," Jerico said. "Remarry. Have children, make friends. Those that survived have a whole life ahead of them."

"Don't tell them that. Right now they dwell in the loss. Some may dwell forever."

Jerico nodded, knowing how right he was. An uncomfortable silence stretched over them. The dark paladin sat on the other side of the fire, and the two stared into the flickering flames.

"With the Citadel's fall, my brethren and the priests have declared war on the paladins of Ashhur," he said at last.

"For what reason?" Jerico asked.

"Is one needed? You know we oppose one another. Centuries ago, Karak and Ashhur warred. It appears it has begun anew."

Jerico felt a pang in his heart as he thought of his friends, and of that terrible image of the Citadel crumbling before an army of the dead. Were they Karak's army? Was that the truth of it?

"Pheus wanted you to kill me," Jerico said.

"I figured that was obvious."

"But you didn't."

"Also obvious."

Jerico smiled despite his exhaustion.

"I owe you my life, Darius. But I guess that, too, is obvious?"

Darius muttered something, then tossed a twig onto the fire.

"What now?" Jerico asked.

"You have to leave. Pheus will return, and he won't come back alone. He's been spreading word all along the river of our newly begun war, and what news he has is not good. Jerico…you may very well be the last of your kind."

"No," Jerico said, shaking his head. He couldn't believe it. It just wasn't possible.

"If not now, then soon. How many of your brethren were at the Citadel when it fell? The few scattered about are young, inexperienced. They'll be hunted down with the full might of Karak. Who can survive that? Our presence is in every nation, felt in every kingdom hall. There is nowhere to run, nowhere to hide."

Jerico felt panic racing through his veins, and he tried to stop it. It couldn't be right. He couldn't be the last. Others would survive, others would fight back…

"Where should I go?" he asked.

"I'd say find safety with your priests, probably the Sanctuary, but that is a long journey south. I don't know if you will make it. Too many will be watching those roads."

"Then what?" Jerico asked. He kicked at the fire, scattering its flame. As it sputtered and died, Darius did his best to offer hope.

"The land north of here is wild, full of bandits. Perhaps there you can hide."

He shook his head. A paladin, hiding? It didn't seem right. It seemed opposite of everything he was.

"Please," Darius said, seeing the hesitation on his face. "I will bear the punishment of this action for the rest of my life. Do not waste it. Do not make me doubt my decision."

It was all too much. Defeated, Jerico nodded.

"So be it," he said. "You are a good friend, and I will honor your wishes. Until I can assure myself of safety, I will find what succor I can in the north. When shall I go?"

"Rest now, then leave in the morning," Darius said, standing. "You must gain as much ground as you can before they come hunting for you. You're strong, Jerico, but those who come after you will be stronger."

Jerico stood, hugged him, then suddenly had a thought.

"A paladin named Pallos passed by here not long ago," he said. "He might return."

"I will warn him if I can," Darius said. "Consider it one last gift for you."

Jerico turned to leave, and as he did, he heard Darius call his name.

"I am sorry for this," he said. "For the Citadel. For my fellows. This is not Karak's desire, and I will show them."

"Thank you," Jerico said, glancing back. "But I fear it is, Darius. If so…what fate awaits you?"

Without waiting for an answer, he returned to the town, where he would sleep late until the morning, gather supplies, and begin his exile in the north.

The troops remained for a few days, making sure no more wolf-men lingered about hoping for a lapse in defenses. Sir Godley vowed to heighten patrols along the river, even if he had to box in the King's ears to do so. Darius listened to it all and faked interest when the time called for it. Truthfully, his mind was elsewhere. He feared for Jerico, and wondered what fate awaited him. But more, he feared the arrival of his brethren, or of the priests. Worst, though, would be the Voice of the Lion, Karak's Hand. Against that feared specter, he wondered if he would even have the courage to speak his defense.

For a while, people asked him about the other paladin's disappearance. Darius always told them Jerico headed south, for he knew they would be questioned when the dark paladins came looking. Whatever bit of disinformation he could sow, the better. Still, when he spoke the lie, he wondered what had happened to his faith. Lies were instruments of chaos, everything he was supposed to stand against. Yet he spoke them freely now to protect a man who should have been his enemy.

Come the ninth night, while he lay in bed staring out the window, he saw the fires in the distance. There was no doubt as to what they were, and who was with them.

Going downstairs, he put a silver coin on the counter. He'd meant to wake Dolores, to thank her for her stay, but she was gone now, and he stayed for free in thanks for his valiant defense. His heart ached at the realization. She'd been a fine innkeeper. Damn the wolves, and damn himself for not being strong enough to protect her.

"Whatever fate you found in eternity, I hope it is pleasant," he said to the quiet night air.

He dressed in his armor, taking time to polish it well in the candle light. No hurry, not for him. Not for what would most likely be his last night on Dezrel. When finished, he cleaned his sword, sharpened it with a whetstone, and then sheathed it across his back. Finished, he knelt at the door of the inn and offered Karak a prayer.

"I have done what I thought was right. I have stood against chaos in the only way I knew how. Give me the strength to show them. Give me the words to speak the truth of your will to those who should know better."

A chill touched his shoulder, and he knew not what to think of it. Deciding enough was enough, he trudged north, to where the three of the Tribunal waited.

16

The light was actually of three torches staked into the ground, and they burned bright as he approached. Darius wished they had chosen a spot closer to the river. At least the soft sound of it flowing along would have brought him some measure of peace. As it was, he had only the wind to keep him company on the walk there, and it was an unpleasant howl through the scattered trees.

Three men waited for him, standing in the gaps between the torches, which formed a triangle. One stepped aside and gestured for Darius to enter. He did.

"I feared you would reject a chance to appear before the Tribunal," Pheus said, his features looking grim in the torchlight.

"I have done no wrong," Darius said. "Why would I fear such a trial?"

Pheus gave no answer.

Darius looked to the other two men. They were paladins of Karak, their black armor almost shimmering in the light of the torches. He recognized both. One was a younger warrior named Nevek, there most likely because he was in the vicinity when the Tribunal was called. He appeared calm, but his eyes belied his nervousness. Darius felt insulted to have one such as him be considered his judge. The man barely had stubble on his chin. The other was an older paladin named Lars, wise and skilled in battle. His faith, in particular, was above question.

"We have heard troubling reports of your actions here in Durham," Lars said. His voice was a deep baritone, and it carried authority. Darius turned to him, trying to ignore the growing feeling of claustrophobia. No matter where he turned, there he would face the eyes of an accuser, so he focused on Lars, who would clearly be the one in charge of the Tribunal.

"My actions were just," Darius replied. "I followed the will of Karak, and I trust this Tribunal to realize that before this night's end."

"Is that so?" Pheus asked. "You threatened my life, the life of both brother and superior. How might you justify that?"

"I too would like to hear an answer," Lars said. "Even if you were on the side of right in your disagreement, I wonder how you could justify such actions."

"We must ever be vigilant against the chaos within ourselves, and our own ranks," Darius said, holding his head high. "Pheus's actions were born of betrayal and hatred, clear enemies of Order."

"You'd dare speak against my name?" Pheus asked.

"Quiet," Lars said, lifting a hand. "There is some truth to this, Darius, though you should have let this matter come to a Tribunal if you felt that the case."

Darius shrugged his shoulders.

"I drew no blood, and I did not expect to. Pheus honored my wishes, as I thought he would."

The priest glared.

"You threatened an unarmed priest, you coward," Nevek said. "You should be hanged!"

"Quiet, Nevek," said Lars. "It is not your place to speak. No judgments are to be made until every last word is spoken. Darius, you were told to execute the paladin of Ashhur, the one known as Jerico. You refused. Tell me why."

Darius took a deep breath. Why did he? The vision of Karak flowed through him, and he saw himself bleeding before the paladin. His life depended on it, yet he had spared him. Was it really friendship?

"Jerico protected the village from the wolf-men," he said. "He stood side by side with me and saved the lives of many men, women, and children. Killing him would have cost me my own life, and theirs as well. Is our mission not to save these people from the chaos of this world? How could I strike down an ally? It makes no sense. It is not the will of Karak. Above all…" He knew he might be hanging himself here, but he had to say it. He had to speak the truth. "Above all, he was my friend. I will not slay a friend, betray his trust, just because he is part of a scattered, broken remnant of Ashhur. We will achieve victory over them through the truth of our words, and the justice of our actions. Not through murder. Not through cowardice."

The three of the Tribunal fell silent as he spoke his last. The wind howled, and Darius thought that perhaps he had won them over. Nevek still looked petulant, but he was young and would abide by the opinions of the others. Pheus was still angry, that much he could tell. It all fell on Lars. The man stroked his neatly-trimmed beard, the two staring eye to eye as he thought.

"You truly believe you do the will of Karak," he said. "Of that, I am certain. But the most dangerous to our cause are those who would disobey every tenet of our belief, all the while certain they understand the real truth. Draw your sword, Darius. Let us see Karak's judgment in this. Let us see how strongly he rewards your faith."

Darius grinned. He had them. His belief in Karak had never been stronger. This was his will. His desire. Drawing his greatsword, he held it before them, to let them see its dark flame.

But there was no fire.

"No," Darius whispered. It couldn't be. Nevek laughed. Pheus grinned. Lars shook his head, clearly saddened. But it couldn't be. It made no sense. Darius felt his knees go weak. The eyes of his brethren were upon him, and he suddenly hated them, hated them more than anything. He wanted to escape. He wanted them gone. His head bowed, as if he could no longer bear the weight. His god, the god he had worshipped all his life, had abandoned him. Because of his disobedience. Because of his protection of the weak.

Because of Jerico.

"You understand what must be done," Lars said. "To threaten one of our own, and be rejected by Karak, leaves only one fate."

Slowly, Darius nodded his head. Lars drew his sword, a heavy blade he wielded with one hand. Its dark fire was great, greater than it had ever burned for Darius. He watched as Lars pulled it back, preparing the swing. Pheus looked satisfied beyond measure. Nevek was still grinning. In and out, Darius breathed. Waiting for the sword to fall.

When it did, he shifted to the side and swung. His sword slashed through Pheus's throat, spilling blood in a wild arc. Continuing his turn, Darius focused on Lars, knowing him the greatest threat. By the time Nevek had even drawn his sword, Darius had cut down the elder paladin, blood gushing from a deep wound in his side.

Nevek screamed something unintelligible but full of hate. Darius cut off his head.

The sudden silence felt like thunder. Standing in the center, Darius looked upon the three dead bodies, still in position between the triangle formation of torches.

"I refuse your judgment," he told the corpses. "For if Karak abandons me, then I will abandon him."

It seemed a coming storm mocked his words with a clap of thunder. His blood chilled. To his left, he heard the soft sound of laughter.

"Abandoned?" said a man, his voice deep. "Is that what you think you are?"

The man stepped into the light of the torches. A lump swelled in Darius's throat. It couldn't be. The man's eyes shone red, as if behind his irises burned a constant fire. He was robed in black, his skin pale and stretched thin across his bones. The man's face, however, was in constant, subtle movement. If he stared hard enough, Darius could see the man's brows thicken, his nose shorten, his lips lift or lower to adapt to the new visage. Always the eyes remained the same.

"Do you know who I am?" asked the man with the ever-changing face.

"I do. Your name was spoken of in both fear and reverence in the Stronghold."

"Tell me, what name do they know me as there?"

Darius lifted his sword.

"You are the Voice of the Lion, his word made flesh."

The man laughed. The sound made Darius want to turn and run.

"It has been many years since I was called by that title. I am Velixar, fallen paladin. I thought to witness your execution for a bit of amusement, but instead find myself watching a far greater surprise. A paladin, lacking the strength of Karak, still takes down two of his brethren, plus a priest? How surprising. How *interesting*."

"Stay back," Darius said, shifting his sword to aim the tip at Velixar's throat. Velixar's eyes sparkled with amusement.

"Or what? You will call down the thunder of Karak? You will pierce me with a blade of simple metal? The blood in my veins has not flowed in centuries. The air in my lungs moves to speak, and nothing else. I am Karak's prophet to this chaotic world. Do you think you have a chance to defeat someone such as I?"

"Willing to try."

Darius stepped close and swung. The blade felt heavier in his arms, the strength gifted to him by Karak long vanished. Still, it should have cleaved right through Velixar's head, sent it rolling to the dirt where he could give it a well-deserved kick. Instead, the man raised a hand, whispered a word, and then grinned. The blade struck his fingers as if they were stone. The shock reverberated up his arm, made his elbows and wrists throb with pain.

"Foolish man."

Black lightning flowed up the blade and into his arms. Darius screamed, and he felt his muscles spasm. When he hit the ground, he writhed there, unable to drop the hilt of his sword. He opened his mouth to cry out, but he could make no sound. All at once, the pain stopped, and he lay there gasping for air.

"You said you know who I am, yet you dare attack anyway? You know nothing, stupid boy."

"Kill me," Darius said, his voice croaking. "Just do it, damn you."

"You are the damned, not me, Darius. But I am not here to kill you."

"Then what?"

Velixar knelt beside him. Darius stared into his eyes, feeling lost within their fanatical fire. The pale man's hand touched his face, and it was cold.

"You are lost," Velixar whispered. "Your god has not abandoned you. You have abandoned your god. You fell to weakness, gave in to folly, and believed the lies of the enemy. But your *faith*, Darius, your faith is still incredible. Even now it cries out to be forgiven. Even now, you wish you had been right, that you could still feel Karak's embrace."

"All I feel is hatred."

Velixar stood, and it seemed the very night gathered about him, worshipping his power.

"I am here, and I offer you my hand. Atone for the sins you have committed. Become my wayward son returned home. I have much I can teach you, and much for you to do."

Darius tried to think, to listen to his heart. What did he believe? What did he want?

"I have seen Karak's truth," he said at last. "I have seen the murder he would have me do. You will not teach me. I refuse."

Velixar's lips curled into a smile.

"You damn fool," he said. "You do not have a choice. Whether you desire it or not, your soul will be redeemed."

Down came the black lightning. It touched his eyes, his throat, his hands, and his heart. As he lay there, his scream pierced the night, and for the first time, Darius regretted letting Jerico live. The pain went on and on. Time lost meaning. Tears ran down his face, and he felt he would do anything to make the torture stop. But it continued, and he could not beg, not plead, only scream out his agony. When it finally did stop, he collapsed once more, and amid the ringing of his ears he heard Karak's prophet laugh.

"You will slay the paladin of Ashhur. You will kill your friend. Only then, when you have placed Karak above all things, will you finally understand. And you will understand. You will learn. You are a part of a game, a simple piece, but I will not lose you to Ashhur. This must be done on your own, though. I will not force you back to Karak. No, I have seen your fate, Darius. You will come to me, of your own free will, and beg for guidance. I will always be near, watching, listening, and come that time, I will be there for you, lost paladin."

And then he was gone. For a long while, Darius lay there, waiting for his strength to return. When it did, he staggered back to town, gathered up his things, and fled.

Epilogue

For several days Jerico traveled along the river. Using a small knife and slender branch he formed a spear, and he ate fish some nights. He avoided the first few villages he encountered, worried they would be the first places checked when his pursuers realized he had left. Assuming he had pursuers. It would be a strange thing to lie about, but Darius might have had his reasons. Still, the image of the falling Citadel haunted him, and if Karak were truly behind it, it was no stretch to believe the dark god's followers had declared war against his very existence. The priest's actions certainly confirmed it.

When his provisions at last ran low, he hid his armor in a copse of trees and traveled into a small village wearing only his trousers, shirt, and the platemail's padded undershirt.

"Heading south?" asked the shopkeep as Jerico paid him for the dried meat and nuts.

"North, actually."

The man turned to the side and spat between his bucked teeth.

"Not a good idea. Lotta men been gathering arms against lord Hemman, calling him lawless, but they's just as lawless as him. Not a safe time to be traveling, unless you want to be heading into the far north naked as the day you was born."

"I will stay wary," Jerico said, paying him.

"Hey, you hear about a man named Kaide, you get your ass far away," the shopkeep said as he was leaving. "He's a cannibal, they say, and he's got a mad wizard as a pet. Uses the blood of virgins to cast his spells is what I hear! Stay safe from where his bandits are roaming!"

Jerico promised he would.

Once he was dressed in his armor, he packed up the food, filled his waterskins at the river, and continued north. Steadily the land grew wilder. Where once he might have traveled a day to reach the next town, it soon took two, then three. All the while he avoided people best he could, removing his armor when he did have to enter a village. At last he arrived in the true north, much of it winter trees growing in enormous stretches at the feet of the Kala Mountains. It was there he thought he'd have the best chance to hide.

Several weeks after the wolves' attack, he walked along one of the few trade routes leading toward the mining villages. His pack was light, and his stomach grumbled, but he felt content. The woods were a vibrant green, despite the approaching winter. The chill air felt fine on his skin, which was slick with sweat from the many hours of walking. There was a storm approaching, though, and he felt a calm warning of Ashhur in the back of his mind.

"Not alone, am I?" he chuckled. "Well, let's see how brave they are."

He shifted his arm so he had a better grip on his shield. A single tug and he'd have it at the ready. It'd be a brave band of bandits that would assault a man in full platemail. What weapons could they possibly have that might punch through, or be long enough to find the gaps in his armor? He caught sight of eyes watching him from the trees, and bird-calls sounded, birds that should have already flown south. Still, another hour passed, and no one revealed themselves. He thought himself free, but still Ashhur called warning.

Up ahead he saw an elderly man walking with a cane. The top of his head was bald, the rest of his hair a pale white. His back was bent, and in his free hand he carried a satchel.

"It is a long road to walk alone," Jerico said, calling out to him. "Care for some company?"

"I'm not alone, young man," the man said, turning toward him. He lifted his staff, and the end shimmered. Cursing, Jerico pulled his shield free, and it burst with blue-white light. That light faded for a moment, then resumed, absorbing the invisible spell.

"An interesting trick," the old man said. He stood with his back no longer bent, and his voice was firm, belying the age he showed. "Maybe you can explain that later."

"I think I'll be going on my way instead."

The old man laughed.

"I think not."

Nets dropped from high above his head, cast by men hiding in the trees. Jerico dodged one, but the second fell upon him, its ends heavily weighted. He pulled at it, swinging his mace in hopes of knocking himself free. The old man's staff shimmered again, and this time his shield was not able to save him. Drowsiness flowed through his veins, making his muscles ache as if he'd just sprinted for miles. Every exertion felt like it would be his last. Whispering prayers to Ashhur, he tried to fight off the spell, but then came the clubs. At least ten bandits descended upon him, bludgeoning him with thick branches of wood stripped of their bark.

As one blow struck his head, he collapsed, his vision swirling with red and black. More blows rained down, most hitting his armor, but some still bruising his flesh. All sound came as if from a distant room.

"Enough," someone said. Jerico looked up, the effort nearly beyond his abilities. He saw a young man in a ponytail frowning down at him.

"You're a paladin, aren't you?" asked this man.

"Why...does it matter...?"

His head hit the ground, lying on a bed of pine needles. Blood trickled from his ear, along his chin, and down his neck.

"What you thinking, Kaide?" asked the old man.

For a long moment, silence. Then came the voice of the second man.

"We have no choice. Take him."

Arms grabbed him, lifting him up still wrapped in the net. As Jerico stared through the gaps, he saw a wrinkled hand wave before his eyes, and then he saw no more.

A Note From the Author:

Welcome to the bit at the end, where I ramble, and you either wish there was more to read, or reflect on how you just wasted your time and money. Hopefully it is the former, but hey, if you're the latter: sorry man, I tried. My original attempts at novel writing (serious attempts, not counting my blatantly plagiarized bastard combination of Chronotrigger and Final Fantasy 2 I concocted in the 5th grade) began in Creative Writing in High School. I've always been a big fan of paladins, and I created a lengthy set of stories throughout my senior year involving Lathaar of the Citadel, last of his kind. I still have those stories in a shoebox, where they'll probably stay considering how painfully written they are. Still, I've always wanted to tell their stories, Lathaar and his newly introduced fellow survivor, Jerico, and this series is it.

I'm starting out with Jerico. People seem to enjoy him more. He's humorous, different, and has a big glowy shield. What's not to like? The main goal of this series is to showcase these paladins. I'll bounce between them, and back and forth through time (but don't worry, the next book will finish up Darius and Jerico; I won't leave you hanging). We'll see the fall of the Citadel, Lathaar's battle with the demon Darakken, his meeting of the demi-goddess Mira, and maybe another here or there when the ideas come. These books won't be as sequential as the Half-Orc novels were, so consider this an experiment on my part. Will it succeed or fail? That's entirely up to you, dear reader. If you're entertained, I'll consider said experiment a success.

Thank you, Daniel, for the inspiration for Jerico and his shield. Thank you Derek for the edits, Peter Ortiz for the sexy cover, and T. M. Roy for the overall design. Last of all, thank you reader for sticking with me to the end. The nights got a bit dark, and the wolves had their time to feast, but the day's come, and the Paladins of both Karak and Ashhur still stand. If you want to contact me, feel free to email me at ddalglish@yahoo.com. You can also become a fan at www.facebook.com/thehalforcs or also visit my website at ddalglish.com.

David Dalglish
May 31, 2011